So we wanted a family, but it had to be right. We got lucky because Ben was brought back, and that night Lola made all six of us one family: James, Edmund, Ben, Al-Willie, Lola and me. None of us had parents.

Lola had just turned eighteen, had this really fantastic job and could leave St. Theresa's legally any time. But who was going to let us younger kids be adopted by an eighteen-year-old? I knew the answer to that one: nobody.

We had to sneak out. We didn't have money worries because of Lola's job, so it was just a matter of getting past the gate and finding a new place where we could all live happily ever after.

JUDIE ANGELL lives in South Salem, New York, with her husband, who is a musician, and their two sons. She is the author of *In Summertime It's Tuffy*, *Ronnie and Rosey*, *Tina Gogo*, *A Word from Our Sponsor*, and *Secret Selves*, also available in Laurel-Leaf editions.

DEAR LOLA

or How to Build Your Own Family

■■■■■■■■■■■■■■■■■■■■■■■■■■

A Tale by Judie Angell

LAUREL-LEAF BOOKS bring together under a single imprint outstanding works of fiction and nonfiction particularly suitable for young adult readers, both in and out of the classroom. Charles F. Reasoner, Professor Emeritus of Children's Literature and Reading, New York University, is consultant to this series.

Published by
Dell Publishing Co., Inc.
1 Dag Hammarskjold Plaza
New York, New York 10017

Special thanks to Jerome Blitzer of Angell & Blitzer,
Attorneys at Law, New York-J.A.

For Sandy,
who could be all of the Benikers,
with love

Laurel-Leaf Library ® TM 766734,
Dell Publishing Co., Inc.

ISBN: 0-440-91787-5

RL: 4.6

Book Club Edition

Reprinted by arrangement with Bradbury Press, Inc.

Printed in the United States of America
First Laurel-Leaf printing—March 1982
Fourth Laurel-Leaf printing—December 1984

1

"Pssssss! Annie!"

I was having a dream. It was terrific. It was about my house: three stories tall, with an attic and a porch. With columns in front. And my own room. And a yard. And a vegetable garden. I hate vegetables but I've always wanted to grow a garden of my own . . .

"Annie! Wake up!"

"Go away," I mumbled. I hate it when my dreams get interrupted. If they're good ones.

"No, Annie, listen: Ben's back. They just brought him in. We have to go *now!*"

I opened my eyes and there was Lola crouched by my bed. I forgot my dream. "Ben's back?" I whispered.

"Yeah. I was in the kitchen when Sister Edwina

came in carrying him. He was asleep," Lola whispered back.

"Well, gee, that's good timing because the rest of us are all here now . . ."

"I know. But Edmund's due to go out again tomorrow . . . We have to move fast."

I bit my lower lip. "Yeah. Edmund. Right. I forgot about that."

"We're going tonight. You get Al-Willie and Edmund. I'll get James and Ben, and we'll all meet by the back gate near the gym in about"—Lola held up my little alarm clock in the moonlight—"fifteen minutes. Don't take much. We can buy everything we need as we go."

"Okay. But Lola?"

"What?"

"I get to pick out the house," I said firmly.

"Annie, look, let's worry about one thing at a time."

"No, I mean it, Lola, the house has to be right or I'm not going."

Lola chucked me under the chin. "Okay, Annie. You have to like the house or we don't get it."

"Deal," I said and got up.

There were about two hundred and fifty kids at St. Theresa's Home and School. Some of us got put up for adoption, some of us were foster kids, and some kids went back to their real parents—but everybody lived at St. Theresa's between jobs, so to speak. They did have a school there and the rooms they gave us were kind of nice . . . It wasn't really a bad deal. The thing is, most kids wanted permanent families. Except for six of us.

We wanted a permanent family too, only it couldn't be just *any* family because we were pretty fussy. We had certain conditions that had to be met.

Al-Willie and I were always turning up back at St. Theresa's because we made a sacred vow never to be split up. And they were always splitting us because it seemed nobody ever wanted a *pair* of kids, only *one* kid. Especially when you're as old as ten. So we were so bad in our separate homes that nobody would keep us. After all, we made the vow in our own blood with a penknife, and since our blood is the same anyway because we're twins, it was double protection, mixing outer blood with inner blood and the vow had to be kept.

Ben was only five and he was so young he might have been happy anywhere except he had this problem. Sister Edwina called it an oral fixation. That just means Ben would eat anything he got his hands on, like paper clips or little toys or Scotch tape or anything like that. If he was at St. Theresa's at Christmas time, he'd eat all the ornaments off the tree. So the teachers and aides would decorate the tree starting from about three-quarters up from the bottom so Ben couldn't reach anything. It sure looked weird. Well, none of the families Ben was placed with were really too thrilled with that kind of stuff and everybody got tired of rushing him to the hospital to have his stomach pumped. All Ben wanted was to get back to St. Theresa's where everybody was used to him and left him alone.

James was thirteen. He wouldn't come out of his room. Not ever. People don't like it when you live with them and you don't come out of your room, so James never found a good place.

Edmund was nine. He hated every place they put him. Sometimes he had good reason, sometimes he couldn't explain why. He said later that no place made him feel as good as he felt with the rest of us five back at St. Theresa's and that was probably it, since we realized that's how we felt, too.

What Edmund did was to throw these real wild tantrums pretty regularly, as if he had a schedule. Twice a day, before meals. Once at night, but not if anyone was still up and could deal with it. Everybody had to be asleep. I saw Edmund throw a real beauty as one couple was about to take him home. Sister Rose Maria had dressed him in this dumb sailor suit and just when the lady was bending over to muss his hair and pinch his cheek, he ripped off the sailor suit, piece by piece, until he was standing there with nothing on except one sock. Then he started to scream at the top of his lungs. That man and lady took off like someone had set a bomb off under their feet.

Edmund's favorite, when a foster family didn't send him back to St. Theresa's fast enough to suit him, was to pull one of these nude scenes in a public place, like a supermarket or the local library or maybe a bowling alley. That usually did it.

So we wanted a family, but it had to be right. We got lucky because Ben was brought back, and that night Lola made all six of us one family: James, Edmund, Ben, Al-Willie, Lola and me. None of us had parents.

Lola had just turned eighteen, had this really fantastic job and could leave St. Theresa's legally any time. But who was going to let us younger kids be adopted by an eighteen year old? I knew the answer to that one: nobody.

We had to sneak out. We didn't have money worries because of Lola's job, so it was just a matter of getting past the gate and finding a new place where we could all live happily ever after.

Lola's real name is Arthur Beniker. Us kids called him Lola because of the terrific job he got with this syndicated column called "Dear Lola." People with problems would send him letters and he'd answer them in the newspaper. That's why it didn't matter where he lived, he just mailed in his column every day and it got printed in newspapers all over the country. And he just told the newspaper people which post office box to send his money to, along with the letters people wrote him.

Nobody knew when he started the column that

he was a seventeen-year-old boy, living most of the time at St. Theresa's Home and School. He says they figured he was a little white-haired old lady with a lot of years behind her. But Lola says that a boy who never even had a place to sleep two nights in a row till he got to St. Theresa's knows a whole lot about problems and feelings. I guess he's right because he's always known a lot about all our problems and helped us a lot. Right from the start.

Al-Willie and Edmund and I got to the back gate first and we waited and waited. I was getting sleepy and I wondered if something had gone wrong. Finally Edmund curled up on the grass next to the cyclone fence and did go to sleep and I was just about to call it quits myself, when Lola showed up carrying Ben, with James about twenty yards behind them.

"I'm sorry, kids," Lola said, panting. "I couldn't get James out."

That was nothing new. James wouldn't even come out for meals. They had to leave a tray outside his door.

"But he's here . . . Come *on*, James!" Lola said over his shoulder in a sharp whisper.

"How'd you get him out?" I asked.

"I told him he could have a room to himself in our house," Lola said. "He wouldn't have to share, it'd be all his."

"And he could stay in it?" Al-Willie asked.

10

"Sure he could, if he wants to," Lola said. "Good. Here he is. Now let's go. Oh, boy . . ."

"What's wrong?" I asked.

"The top button of my jacket's missing. Ben probably ate it."

"Well, he's asleep now . . . Just watch him when he wakes up."

There was nothing blocking the gate and we just walked out. Lola still carried Ben; Al-Willie and I held Edmund's hand between us; and James walked behind us all.

2

St. Theresa's wasn't exactly in a city, but it wasn't a small town, either, and it wasn't really country-like. We wanted to live in the country, where nobody would pay much attention to us and we could live in a house all by ourselves and grow our own stuff and maybe have a cow or something so we'd have milk. Lola figured he had the money for the down payment but the thing was to get as far away from St. Theresa's as we could so we'd never get picked up and sent back there. It's not that St. Theresa's was a bad place. It's just that it wasn't *our* place. So we headed west. I don't know how Lola knew which was west, but I didn't worry about it. He knew.

We walked a lot. I mean a lot. If it was nice out. It was April and warm but not hot so it wasn't bad. At night we slept outside or in someone's garage if it was far enough from their house. I liked best sleeping in little parks, especially if there was a pond or a stream and you could hear the water while you were dozing off.

When it rained, we spent the day in a library. The first time we did it I thought I'd really be bored, but it was so great I found that I was hoping for rain when I woke up the next day.

Lola read to us. Most of the time he'd pick short stories, usually by one author for a day. My favorite authors were Edgar Allan Poe and Mark Twain. Al-Willie *loved* Edgar Allan Poe, especially *The Pit and the Pendulum.* Edmund liked Washington Irving. James never said what he liked best, he just kind of sat off by himself and listened. Ben napped mostly and one of us would read picture books to him when Lola was finished and reading by himself. I taught Ben his alphabet. I mean, he already knew the letters from St. Theresa's but I showed him how you could put letters together to make words.

Lola did something else that was good in the libraries—he'd start a book in one library and then do another chapter in the next town library we came to. It was fun. We'd beg him to continue and he'd just smile and close up the book and say he'd read more next time. He did that with a book called *Catcher in the Rye* and we all liked it a lot.

Lola had a map. He didn't know exactly where

we'd end up but he knew which way we were going, so he'd make sure we hit certain towns on the way. This was so he could let the people know where to send all his mail, care of the post office, and he'd be sure to pick it up and answer it and send in his columns in advance. In those towns, we'd stay at motels.

"Oh, boy! A TV!" Al-Willie cried when we saw our first room.

"No TV," Lola said quietly. "At least not all the time."

"Why?"

"Because you're missing school and you have to keep up with your studies. And also because there are things you'll all have to know for when we have our own house."

"Like what?" I asked.

"Like electricity. And plumbing."

We spent days in motels reading how-to books. Lola would take James with him to the post office to pick up his cartons of mail. They they'd come back and James and Lola would go to their own rooms to read. Lola shared his room with Ben. Al-Willie and Edmund and I shared a room, and James had his own.

We were all Lola's assistants but James was his real one. He'd read letters and decide which ones would be right for the column and which ones wouldn't. Lola showed him how to pick letters that a lot of people could relate to, but occasionally Lola wanted a real unusual problem to vary the column. Mainly, though, James could pick letters that interested him and Lola would check them over. James liked it because he got to spend time all by himself and still do something useful. Lola liked it because it really helped him. One day, James got the idea of using rubber stamps that said YES and NO to put on the envelopes to save time. Lola thought that was a great idea. We had a nice routine worked out.

Sometimes we'd have a real big room, like at the Bide-Your-Time Motel, and then we'd all be reading and writing together . . . like a big study hall. One time we were all together, except James who was next door, and we were all quiet and everything when Lola looked up from his work.

"Annie?"

"Hm?"

"What're you reading?"

"This book you gave me. *Handy Hints on Help in the Home.* I'm up to 'How to Fix a Clogged Sink.' "

"Good. Can you fix one?"

"Sure. What're *you* reading?"

"*Custody Battles: An Anchor for the Children* and, um, *Single Parenting* and . . . *A Child's Civil Rights* . . ."

"That sounds like a good one," I said. "How come you're reading all that stuff?"

"Personal and professional reasons," he said. "I

have to know what to do about you, and I have to research all the time. For the column."

I looked at my plumbing book. "So studying isn't just for school, is it?"

"For school? Studying and reading isn't for school, Annie. It's for *you*. And for *us*. So pick up that book again and start learning."

"Yeah, okay." I turned the page. "I'm up to 'toilets' now."

"Good."

"Blagh."

Al-Willie stole a lot of the food we ate. Lola wanted to buy it and tried to, but Al-Willie got a big kick out of stealing it. Lola said we'd be in bad trouble if Al-Willie got caught but he wouldn't quit.

One time after I saw him nearly get seen ripping off a whole ham, I grabbed him outside. "Al-Willie, if you get caught," I said, pushing his shoulders up against the wall, "I'm breaking our pact and we'll be split up for-*ever!*"

"No, Annie, listen . . ." he began. I could tell he was really upset because he started digging holes in the ham with his fingers. I took the ham away. "It's only that I want to do my share, too. You know?" he said. "If we're supposed to be a real family, then what's *my* job?"

Boy, he had me. I didn't know what to say. Slowly we started to walk to the park where we had left the others. Al-Willie's idea about doing his share sounded pretty good to me but the way he picked to do it wasn't so good.

We talked it over with Lola who said that we'd all have a proper share to contribute once we got to where we were going and that up until then, the best thing we could do was just to stick together and not draw too much attention to ourselves.

And that's what we did until the end of June, when we finally found Sweet River.

3

It seemed just like what we were looking for. Lola found the house one day while he and James were hitching back to our motel with their sacks of mail. It was on a dirt road with lots of land around it and not too many other houses nearby. It wasn't three stories unless you counted the crawl-space attic, but it did have a real front porch with columns—skinnier than the ones in my dreams, but okay—and best of all, it was deserted. Lola found out that the people who owned it had to leave before they could sell it and it had been all alone with no one living in it for about a year. Lola said that was terrific because it sat so long it got rundown, which made the price lower. The people were anxious to sell and we were anxious to buy, so Lola bought it.

Then we really found out why Lola made us read all those books in the libraries and motels:

"Annie!"

"What, Edmund?"

"All the water stays in the sink. It won't go down when I jiggle the thing-a-ma-gunk!"

"Coming!" I climbed down off the ladder where I'd been painting the molding in the kitchen. "Which bathroom are you in?"

"Up here! The one near James's room!"

I found him. There're four bathrooms in the house. "Now what is it you were jiggling?"

"This."

"The stopper. You've pulled it out."

"I know, but still the water won't go down."

"Okay, you go get me a wire hanger and the plunger out of Lola's bathroom. Then get Al-Willie to take over the painting in the kitchen and you take over the stove scrubbing from *him.*"

"But I was supposed to scrub out the bathrooms!"

"I'll do the bathrooms. There's been something wrong with the plumbing in each one so far. So we'll change jobs."

"Al-Willie!"

"Yeah?"

"Where are you?"

"That you, Lola?"

"Yeah!"

"Where are *you?*"

"Ben and Edmund's room! The overhead light just blew in here!"

"Change the bulb!"

"I did, smarty! It's not the bulb!"

"Okay, I'm coming! Annie!"

"What?"

"Where are you?"

"Downstairs bathroom!"

"What did you do with my splicer?"

"It's on the shelf in your room! What'd you do with the tank ball?"

"What tank ball?"

"The one I asked you to buy in the hardware store yesterday!"

"Oh! I didn't buy it. It was plastic."

"*So what?*"

"So you said tank balls are metal!"

"I don't care if it's made of sterling silver! The water'll keep running in this toilet unless we put in a new tank ball!"

"I'll get it later!"

"*Al-Willie!*"

"Coming, Lola!"

"Edmund!"

"What? Gee, you scared me, Annie!"

"Sorry. But look at Ben!"

"Oh, Man . . ." Edmund rushed over to where Ben was putting little screws in his mouth. "Don't,

21

Ben. Hey, I'll make you a sandwich . . ." he said, pinching Ben's mouth open and taking out the screws.

"Come on, Edmund, your job is supposed to be watching him . . ."

"Listen, Annie, that's only one of my jobs, you know . . . If I'm going to be the cook, I have to know what I'm doing, don't I? I was reading this recipe book here . . ."

"Tell you what," I said. "Take Ben outside to the tire swing. Then he can play and you can read the book out there. Okay?"

"Yeah, okay. Here, Ben, here's a sandwich."

Ben said, "If it's that egg salad you made yesterday, I'd rather have the screws . . ."

One day, Edmund called us all down from where we were working.

"Close your eyes," he said, "and then come into the kitchen."

"I can't find the kitchen with my eyes closed," Ben wailed.

"Well, look at the ground, then. This is a surprise!"

"What'd you make, Edmund?" Lola asked. "I don't smell anything . . ."

"It's not what I made. Okay . . . Open your eyes!"

Sitting on the floor was a pink cat.

"What's that?" from Al-Willie, plus a frown.

"It's a cat, dummy," Edmund said. "What'd you think it was?"

"How'd it get here?" Lola asked.

Ben said, "It's *pink!*"

"I don't know how it got here, and it's not pink, it's tan. Can we keep it?" Edmund bent down to pat it. It gave him a sneering look and began licking its paw.

"Well, gee, Edmund . . ." Lola began, "maybe it belongs to somebody."

"It doesn't," Edmund said firmly.

Ben said, "That cat is pink."

Al-Willie said, "I've got to go change a fuse."

"Can't we keep him," Edmund whined through his nose.

"Listen, Edmund, are you going to throw a tantrum if we don't keep him?" I asked.

"No . . ." Edmund said and relaxed his shoulders.

"He can stay as long as he stays," Lola said.

"What do you mean?" Edmund wanted to know.

"If he belongs to someone then he'll go home eventually," Lola said.

"I just gave him a tuna fish sandwich," Edmund said. I looked around. Sure enough, ripped bread was all over the floor in a corner.

"He'll never go home," I said.

Edmund said, "He is home."

The cat stayed. He hung around Edmund when

he wanted food but he took his naps in James's room. He'd scratch on James's door and James would open it and the cat would march in with his tail straight up in the air. He acted like he was proud. He should have been—he was the only one allowed in James's room.

4

We all adopted Lola's name—Beniker. Al-Willie painted the name on the fence outside in the front. We figured it would be a lot easier and we were all one family, anyway. One family. In the Beniker house. I used to have pretend conversations with people, like, "Hi, there. Yes, I'm one of the Benikers that live in the beautiful Beniker house over there . . . We fixed it up ourselves. We're a very close family . . ." It was turning out to be a terrific summer. And then my imaginary conversation turned into a real one.

One day in mid-August, I went into town with Lola. He had bought a new van. Well, it wasn't new, it was used, but it worked just fine. Anyway we went into town because Lola's mail was due in and we needed some stuff at the hardware store.

We were going to paint Ben and Edmund's room pale blue. I was picking out paint when a girl came up to me in the aisle. She had on purple jeans and a lavender shirt. I felt funny in my overalls.

She said, "Hi."

"Hi," I said back.

"You live here?" she asked.

"Uh huh. We moved in last month. The big, uh, the house over on the River Road."

"Oh. That one."

I didn't like the way she said "*that* one."

"We've been fixing it up. It looks beautiful, you should see it," I told her.

"How old are you?"

"Ten . . ."

"Thought so. I am, too. You going into fifth grade?"

Something in my stomach turned. I hadn't given any thought to school and didn't want to. School wasn't part of our life.

"Probably won't be going to school," I said and began to bury my nose in paint labels.

"Won't be *going*—" the girl began, but I cut her off.

"But if I did go, I'd be in fifth grade," I said. "Say, you like this color blue?" I didn't care if she liked it or not but I didn't want to talk about school.

"It's okay. What's your name?"

"Annie Beniker."

"Mine's Molly Stamwick. My parents are teachers at the high school."

"Oh."

"My father's a physics teacher. My mother teaches typing."

"That's nice . . ."

"We *thought* someone bought that old house, but we weren't sure . . ."

I sniffed. "Well, we haven't started on the outside, yet. We've mostly been working on the inside. Next month we'll do the outside, then you'll notice how good it looks . . ."

"Who's *we?*" she asked.

"Oh, me and my brothers . . ."

"What about your parents?"

"What about them?" I asked.

Molly Stamwick looked me up and down. "I'm going swimming this afternoon," she said, "with two girls in my class. You, um . . ." She looked at her nails. "You want to come?"

I shrugged. "Thanks, but I can't. I really have too much to do. Around the house. But thanks, anyway . . ."

She looked at me again, up and down, and then she turned and walked away.

" 'Dear Lola: My husband's father has been living with us since his wife passed away five months ago. I don't know what to do with him. He sits around the house all day, never goes anywhere, hardly talks to anyone. We've tried to take

27

him on family outings or out to eat or to the movies, but he just sits like a lump. What do you suggest we do?' Signed *'Fed Up.'* "

Lola put down the letter. "James likes this one for the column because it has to do with different generations living in the same house. Lots of people find that a problem. What do you think?"

"I think he's not with the right family," Al-Willie said.

"Who, the grandfather? But it's *his* family," Lola said.

"But he's not happy in it. He needs to find another one," Al-Willie explained.

Lola stroked his chin.

"Like we did," Edmund piped up. "A family he really wants to be with and that really wants *him.*"

I said, "I bet he misses his wife."

"I bet he does, too, Annie," Lola said. "And I think you're right. He does need a new family. People his own age who understand what he's going through and have been through it themselves. *Fed Up* doesn't say if she's tried any senior citizens' groups. There are some wonderful ones around. Here . . ." Lola began scribbling on a piece of paper.

"What's that?" I asked.

"A note for James. Tell him to answer this letter with the following suggestions and look up the names of the groups we want on my master list."

"Hey!" Ben cried from the floor. "Somebody's out front!"

Sure enough, when we got quiet, there was the sound of the doorbell we'd only heard when one of us got locked out.

"I'll get it," Lola said. "Al-Willie, you take this up to James."

Lola got it, but we were all crowded behind him.

Standing there on the porch were two women. One had on a yellow sleeveless dress and the other one was wearing shorts and a work shirt with the ends tied together over her stomach. The one in the dress was holding a square box.

Lola said, "Uh. Hello."

"Hello," Yellow-dress said. She smiled. "I'm Edith Stamwick and this is Martha McElroy . . ."

Lola nodded.

"We're neighbors of yours?"

Lola nodded again. We just looked.

Edith Stamwick pushed the box at Lola. "This is a pineapple-banana upside-down cake," she said. Lola took the box and looked at it. Al-Willie and I made faces at each other and the box.

The two women looked at each other.

"Is your mother home?" Mrs. Stamwick asked.

Lola said, "This—this is very kind of you, Mrs. Stamwick . . . Mrs. McIntosh . . ."

"McElroy," Mrs. Stamwick interrupted.

"Sorry. Won't you come in, please?" Lola stepped back from the door. I could practically *see* him trying to get himself together.

"Thank you," Mrs. Stamwick said.

Stamwick, I thought. Stamwick. "Oh!" I said out loud.

"Annie?" Lola said, looking at me.

"Uh . . . Stamwick . . . Molly is—you have a daughter, name of Molly?"

"That's right, dear," she said, smiling at me.

"Molly, this girl, she's ten, she talked to me today in the store," I explained.

"Yes . . ." Molly's mother said. "Is your mother home?" Again. The other woman, Mrs. Mackel-something, hadn't said one word.

"We, uh," I began, but Lola pressed down on my shoulder with his fingers.

"We don't have parents, Mrs. Stamwick, our parents died."

"Oh. I'm terribly sorry."

Lola nodded and Al-Willie said, "That's okay."

"Well, then, your legal guardian . . ." Mrs. Stamwick began.

Lola, holding the box with the cake, snapped up like he was standing at attention. "Our guardian?" he repeated. "Oh, you mean our legal guardian!"

"Yes . . ."

"Our *legal*, uh, guardian."

Mrs. Stamwick laughed a little. "Well, yes. What's your name?"

"Arthur Beniker, I'm sorry, I was under the impression you knew our name," Lola said all in one breath. "Yes, well, we live with our . . . grandfather. His wife passed on about five months ago. We lived with both of them. Now we live with just him."

"Oh."

"Yes. He's retired now. Wanted to move out of his old house . . . You know . . . memories . . ."

"Of course."

"These are my brothers, Ben, Al-Willie and Edmund and this is my sister, Annie," Lola said, pointing to us.

Everyone nodded at each other.

"Well," Mrs. Stamwick said, backing toward the door, "we just wanted to say 'Welcome to Sweet River.'"

"That was very nice of you," Lola said.

"Please tell your grandfather we called?"

"Of course . . ."

"Good night . . ."

"'Night," Lola said.

"'Night," from Mrs. Mackel-something.

Al-Willie said, "Gee, she can talk after all," when the door had closed behind them.

Lola said, "Whew," and wiped his forehead. His hands were wet, "Oh, boy . . ." He held the box with the cake away from his body. It was dripping. "Hey, Al-Willie, do something with this, will you?"

Al-Willie took the box and ran for the kitchen. I said, "Our *grandfather?*"

"Yeah, that's it, Annie. I made it up on the spot but now we're stuck with it."

"You got it from that letter, huh?"

"Yeah, but it was a good idea, I think. A poor bereaved old man, retired, keeps to himself, depends on his grandchildren . . ."

". . . But still a guardian," Al-Willie said, coming back into the room.

"Yeah, no one can deal with us being on our own. Just remember the grandfather story if someone asks you. Edmund, you go upstairs and tell James."

"What for?" Edmund asked. "Who's he going to talk to?"

We all went back to working in the house. Lola had been sanding down the floor in the hall, but now he was working at it really hard, straining and sweating.

"Hey!" I said when I passed him. He was rubbing his sore knees. "What's the matter? You look mad."

"I'm not mad, Annie. Just a little worried."

"About those women?"

He nodded. "A little."

"They just brought us a cake is all," I said.

"I know. That was nice, but . . ."

"They were nosing around, weren't they, Lola?"

"Possibly . . ." he said.

"But there's nothing they can do to us."

Lola said, "Right."

"Hey!" came a yell from the kitchen. "Hey, look at this! He loves it!"

We ran in there. Al-Willie was sitting on the kitchen counter, laughing. Edmund was crouched on the floor next to his pink cat, whose head was buried in Mrs. Stamwick's cake box.

"Look at that," Edmund marveled. "That must be some cake!"

"Watch it, Edmund, he might get sick," Lola warned, shaking his head.

"Not him. Not Saint Theresa," Edmund said proudly.

"*Who?*" Al-Willie asked from his perch on the counter.

"Saint Theresa," Edmund said, standing up. "I finally found the right name for him. I tried out a lot, but this is right. He's Saint Theresa, that's who he is."

"Edmund, you can't name him Saint Theresa," Al-Willie said firmly. "It's sacrilegious."

"I don't know what that means and I don't care," Edmund said. "He's my discovery and he joined the family and I can name him what I want. And I want to name him Saint Theresa after the place that . . . The place where . . ."

"The place that brought us together," Lola finished.

Edmund said, "Right. Yeah."

"You can't call him Saint Theresa," I said. "He's a boy."

Edmund said, "I don't care. That's his name, Saint Theresa the Cat."

Al-Willie sighed. "We'll all get punished by the real St. Theresa for naming a mangy, scroungy, boy cat after her . . ."

"Yaaaghh!" We all jumped. It was Edmund screaming. He hadn't screamed like that in a long time.

"Come on!" Lola said suddenly. "It's not worth fighting about. It's not worth one of your tantrums, Edmund . . ."

"It is! He called Saint Theresa mangy and *scroungy—*"

"I'm sorry, I'm sorry," Al-Willie said, finally jumping down from the counter. "Call him what you want, Edmund, I didn't mean to insult him."

So Saint Theresa Beniker officially joined the family.

5

"Psssst! Come on, Annie, wake up!"

"Go away."

"Annie, you have to get up. Ben and Edmund are depending on you and so am I. Besides, you have to get Al-Willie up, too." I kept my eyes closed but I felt the mattress sink as Lola sat down on my bed.

"Why?"

"You know why, Annie. For school."

"School!" I opened my eyes.

"Don't you play dumb with me, Annie Beniker," Lola said, frowning. "I told you last week that I registered you kids and last night I told you you'd have to be up for the bus. Don't you pretend you never heard me . . ."

I buried my face in the pillow. I really had forgotten all about school, or at least what Lola'd said about it. I'd just put it right out of my mind.

"Get your head out of the pillow, Annie. You kids *have* to go to school."

"No. I'm not going," I said. "I've been away from it too long, I'm out of the habit."

Lola smiled. "Don't worry about keeping up, Annie. If anything, you'll be ahead. You've been studying pretty hard ever since we left."

"Come on, Lola, that's *why* we left, isn't it? To do what we want?"

"Annie, listen—we left to be together and we *are* together, but we're not going to do each other much good if we don't learn anything new."

"But we *are* learning. Like you said. We've been studying."

"But that's not enough, Annie. We're not hermits. Besides . . ." He pulled my pillow out from under my head and smacked me on the backside with it. ". . . it's the law!"

"So?"

"So we can't call attention to ourselves by breaking the law. Now you get up and I'll show you what your curriculum's going to be!"

"How do *you* know what my curriculum's going to be?" I demanded.

"Are you kidding? Would I send my family to a school without checking it out first? Now—" he grabbed for the pillow again and grinned—"get up!"

"Okay, Annie and Al-Willie, here's the curriculum sheet I picked up at the school for the fifth grade. Take a look at it." Lola pushed some typed sheets of paper at us across the breakfast table.

Al-Willie said, " Awww . . ."

"What about James?" I asked.

"I'll teach James here."

"That's not fair!"

Lola smiled at me, which made me nervous. "Okay, Annie, okay. You want to stay home and have me for a teacher?"

I nodded, knowing I was walking right into a trap.

"Fine," Lola said.

"Fine?"

"Uh huh. But that means that you stay in your room. Just like James. We'll leave your meals outside your door, just like we do with him. And no going out to play or helping around the house or—"

I stuck my tongue out at him and finished my milk.

"Good girl," Lola said. "What're you doing, Edmund?"

"Packing Saint Theresa's lunch."

"His *lunch?*" from Al-Willie.

"Sure. He's got to eat lunch, too."

"Lola can feed him . . ." Al-Willie said.

"How? He'll be at school. With me," Edmund said.

"You can't take a cat to school," Al-Willie said.

37

He reached across me and pulled a rubber eraser out of Ben's mouth.

"Oh, yes I can," Edmund said quietly.

Lola got up from the table and went over to Edmund. "Edmund, Saint Theresa can't go to school with you."

"Oh, yes he can," Edmund said even more quietly.

"Edmund, he won't be happy in school."

"Well, I won't be happy without him."

"Edmund—"

"*Yaaaaaaaaaaaaaaaagh!*" Edmund screamed.

"Oh, no," I said.

"*Yahgh, Yaghgg!*" Edmund's head was whipping back and forth. We all just stood there and let him get on with it. Pretty soon all his new school clothes were in a heap on the floor and the only thing on his body was a sock.

"Okay," Lola said, finally. "You finished?"

"*Aaaaaaaaaaaghghg!*" Edmund yelled, but he was finished. We could tell. The scream was kind of losing heart.

"Saint Theresa's a cat, Edmund, not a person. He needs to be here, where he can run around. School is for kids. Saint Theresa learns his lessons in the woods. That's *his* job—learning how to be a cat."

"He already knows how to be a cat," Edmund said and sniffed.

"He wouldn't be happy, Edmund. Don't you

38

want him to be happy? If you love someone you want him to be happy," Lola said.

Then Edmund cried, but that was good. It meant his tantrum was over.

The bus stop was at a crossroads just a little way from our house. There were two other kids waiting when we got there. One of them was Molly Stamwick. The other was a little girl about nine, Edmund's age.

"Hello, Annie," Molly said.

"Hello."

"This is my sister, Aurora."

Aurora didn't say anything.

"This is Al-Willie, we're twins," I said. "This is Edmund. This is Ben." I pulled the buckle from his knapsack out of Ben's mouth.

Molly said, "Twins, huh?"

"Yeah."

"How did you like my mother's cake?" Molly asked. "You never said."

"Ummm . . ."

"Saint Theresa liked it a lot," Edmund said, smiling, but before Molly could ask who Saint Theresa was, Ben waddled up to her, yanked a little key chain off her jeans belt and swallowed it.

"Hey!" Molly cried out. "Hey! He ate my housekey! Hey, that little kid ate my housekey! Get it back! You make him give it back!"

Al-Willie started to laugh, but when Molly began shaking Ben, Al-Willie pushed her and she fell down.

"Oh!" Molly shouted in surprise.

Aurora began to laugh. She put her hands over her mouth and turned away so that her older sister wouldn't see her, but when Edmund saw Aurora laughing, he began to laugh, too, and then Aurora couldn't hold it any more and pretty soon, she and Edmund were on the ground like Molly, only Molly wasn't laughing. She was glaring at me.

"What kind of crazy family are you?" she yelled.

Just then the big yellow school bus that none of us saw coming pulled up, raising a whole lot of dust and making Molly Stamwick cough so she couldn't finish yelling.

"Come on, Ben," I said, finally.

Molly was crying. "He ate my key," she said to the bus. "That kid—" her arm stretched out, pointing—"he ate my housekey!"

The bus door opened with a gasping sound and Molly tromped up the steps, dragging Aurora behind her by the wrist. I brushed Ben off and pushed him on the bus. When I climbed on myself, I could see all the kids leaning over each other to stare at us. Nobody was talking.

"They're crazy," Molly said, panting. "They're a crazy new family. With no parents, my mother said, just an old retired grandfather. Probably let's 'em just run around wild . . ." She glomped down in a seat next to a girl with a ponytail. "And that crazy little kid ate my housekey and my parents'll be late today and how are Orie and I supposed to get into the house anyway? That's a crazy bunch, I'm not kidding!" And then she just sat there and gulped air while Al-Willie and Ben and I slunk toward the back. I sat down and put Ben on my lap. Edmund sat down next to Aurora. They were both still giggling. It was the only sound on the bus. All the other kids were so quiet it was eerie. It wasn't a real good beginning.

6

"Well, once you got to school how did it go?" Lola asked that afternoon after we all got back.

"The work wasn't hard but no one talked to us," I answered.

"They whispered," Al-Willie said. "And pointed at us."

Lola rubbed Al-Willie's cheek. "They'll come around after they get to know you. You can handle it. Did you understand your teacher? The work?"

"There wasn't much work. It was only the first day . . ."

"Anyone ask about your parents?"

"Not direct," Al-Willie said.

"Naw," Edmund said.

"Molly told everyone we lived with our grandfather. She said he lets us run wild."

Lola smiled. "Well, we have to stick to that. And if Grandfather's retired and in mourning then that'll explain why nobody ever sees him around. When I registered you for school, I told them he was sick. But still, they made me take the papers home for him to sign and then I brought them back."

"You did?"

"Yeah. So if anyone does ask, you just say he's been sick for a while."

". . . Molly also said it's too bad for me that I have to be the only girl in a house with all those boys. She says that'd make anyone crazy . . ." I said.

"Oh, yeah?" Al-Willie growled. "What does *she* know . . ."

"You're not goin' crazy, are you, Annie?" Edmund asked.

"'Course not. But . . . it might be fun to have another girl . . . What do you think, Lola?"

"Maybe someday, Annie. Right now I've got about all I can handle . . ."

"How out Orie?" Edmund piped up. "Orie's nice. She might be a good sister."

"Who's Orie?" Lola asked.

"Orie Stamwick. She's in my class."

"Aurora," I explained. "Molly's sister."

"She's not like Molly. She's nice," Edmund said.

"But she can't be our sister. She's already got a sister. And a mom and dad," I said.

"Well, I like her," Edmund said and folded his arms.

"Good, I'm glad somebody's made a new friend," Lola said. "Now, here." He handed me a tray with milk and cookies on it. "Take this upstairs for James. Then come down and have your own snack."

There was a letter sticking out from under James's door when I went up. It was one of Lola's and James had written on the envelope, "Read this to the kids." I brought it downstairs and Lola read it to himself and smiled.

"Okay," he said finally. "Sit down and listen to this." We sat down at the kitchen table, which was two card tables pushed together with a tablecloth over them. " 'Dear Lola: I'm eleven years old and I'm a twin. I hate it because my brother does everything better than I do and my parents keep saying why can't I be more like him? He gets good grades in school and I don't and he does chores and I don't and everybody likes him better than me.' Signed, *Miserable Being a Twin.*' "

Al-Willie said, "The kid hates being a twin?"

Lola nodded and Al-Willie shook his head.

"Lola, you going to use it?" I asked. "I mean, you going to put that letter in your column and answer it?"

Lola shrugged his shoulders. "What do *you* think?" he asked. "Think I should?"

45

"Hey, let *us* answer it," I told him. "Al-Willie and me. Who'd know better about being twins than twins?"

"Yeah," Al-Willie said. "I can answer it in about six words."

"Let's answer it, Al-Willie, each by ourselves!" I ran to the drawer where we kept paper and pencils. "Come on. Here, you write the twin a letter and I'll write one."

"Sure. Okay," Al-Willie said. He slid over his paper and licked the end of his pencil. I sat down opposite him and started to write, "Dear Miserable," the way Lola does.

Al-Willie was done in two minutes. Not counting the beginning and end it was six words, just like he said.

Here's what he wrote:

> *Dear Miserable,*
> *Tell your parents to butt out.*
> *Love,*
> *~~Al-Willie~~ I mean Lola*

Mine took a lot longer, but here's what I said:

> *Dear Miserable,*
> *I'm really sorry you're miserable being a twin. I'm a twin and I'm glad because before I got adopted my brother was all I had and I never wanted to be separated from him. No-*

*body ever told me to be more like my brother
and nobody ever told him to be more like me
no matter what we did so I can't understand
why your mom and dad don't let you be just
what you are. But I think they're the ones
who have a problem and not you so maybe
you should tell them to write to Dear Lola.
Meanwhile try to be glad you've got a
brother because not everybody has one.*

*From your friend,
Ann Louise Beniker*

I don't really have a middle name, or if I do I
never knew it, so I made up the "Louise" part because it sounds more real when you have a long
name in a business letter.

We gave our letters to Lola who read them and
nodded a lot to himself.

"Okay," he said finally. "I *will* use this letter in
the column. It's definitely a problem that could
use some resolving. And I'm going to quote both
your letters and say that I've drawn from the very
best possible source—twins about the same age."

"All *right*," Al-Willie said.

Lola slapped him lightly on the shoulder.
"Thanks," he said. "Thanks, Annie."

"Any time," I told him.

7

School got worse. Molly let all the other kids know what she thought of us Benikers. Her being in my class didn't help. She said her folks were mad at us, too, because we never called to thank them for that awful cake and because she and Orie had to break a window to get into their house that first day of school because Ben ate their key, which I was sure tasted better than that old cake!

"I think she sicked her baby brother on me," I heard Molly say to some girls one recess. "Sent him over to grab my key, just like you'd send a dog to fetch!"

"No kidding," one girl said.

"Would I lie? And you know what else, her twin brother tried to beat me up, can you imagine?"

"No! Her *brother*? Al-Willie? I always thought Al-Willie was nice."

"Well, he beats up on girls. Probably afraid of boys his own size."

"I'll kill 'em," Al-Willie said when I told him.

"Al-Willie, hold it," Lola said calmly.

"Why can't I just stay home here and learn my lessons with James and you?" I asked Lola. "I learned as much from you all summer as I could learn in school . . ."

"No, Annie," he said, shaking his head. "First of all, no one knows about James, I didn't register him. And there's no chance of anyone seeing him . . ."

"Even us," Al-Willie said.

"But they know about you and if you don't show up at school, the authorities will be here faster than you could imagine. Besides, it's important for you to go to school and mix with other kids. James is different, you know that. It'd be a disaster to try to put him in with other kids now. Being here with us is the best thing for him. He's with other people who care about him . . . But he can be alone, too, and for James that's important."

"Yeah, okay," I said. "But what if they jump me from behind or something?"

"I'll *kill* 'em!" Al-Willie screamed.

* * *

They didn't jump me from behind or anything like that, but they did talk about us from behind. We got our first message on how much they were talking when Al-Willie and I went to pick up Lola's mail around the end of September. We'd been getting the mail at the Sweet River Post Office since the beginning of June, even before we moved into our house, and nobody ever said anything. Usually there were two or three people working there, the postmaster, Mr. Ward, and his wife and, some afternoons, a woman named Greta. That day Al-Willie and I went, all three were there.

Mr. Ward handed over two boxes to us, and as we were putting them in the canvas sacks we always used to carry the mail, he snorted, "Humph," while he bent over his counter to watch us.

I looked up and said, "Huh?"

"Just wondering about this stuff you get so regular," Mr. Ward said. "None of my business, a-course . . ."

"Right," Al-Willie said, pulling the string on his sack. I jabbed him.

"What do you mean, Mr. Ward?" I asked as nicely as I could.

"Well . . . boxes, envelopes . . . bulky . . . always for Mr. Arthur Beniker . . . All on the up and up, is it?"

Al-Willie got that look in his eye that means "Watch it!" but I jabbed him again.

51

"Why, sure, Mr. Ward. Just . . . plain stuff," I said.

Mr. Ward put his elbows up on the counter. "Couple years ago," he said, talking while he exhaled, "feller sent a bomb through the mail. Box just about the size of those there." He nodded his head at our sacks. "Felt the same way when you shook it, too. I remember."

"You shake our mail?" Al-Willie asked.

"Don't get that look, young man, I'm not prying. I can't help but feel it when I'm sorting the mail out, y'know. Just want to make sure there's no shenanigans going on in our little town. It's a small town, y'know."

"Well, we've been getting Lo—I mean, Arthur's—mail now for quite a while . . . If it was a bomb I guess it would have gone off by now," I said.

"I don't know, young lady," Mr. Ward said, glaring at me suddenly. "But we like to know just what's going on in our town here. It's the job of public officials like me to make sure everything's on the up and up."

"Well, we're on the up and up," I said. "You shouldn't believe gossip started by silly girls."

I knew he was still looking at me, even though I turned my back and walked out.

"Is that what you think?" Al-Willie said when we were outside. "Molly Stamwick and that bunch spread it around that we're sending bombs through the mail?"

"Oh, I don't know if she said that exactly . . . But she's always talking about us. And I bet her parents are, too. It sure is a small town!"

"But that's what we wanted," Al-Willie said. "A small town!"

Lola didn't like what I told him when we got home, but no one had any idea about what to do.

"I just wanted us to live quiet, peaceful lives here for a while," Lola said. "Well . . . guess I'll have to be really nice to everybody when I go into town."

"Smile a lot," I suggested.

"Right."

There was a thump on the ceiling, which we knew was James banging his shoe. That was the way he let Lola know he was through with his day's work. Saint Theresa, who was playing with a ball of string on the floor, never got used to that thump and leaped into the air with a yowl, leaving the ball of string for Ben, who wanted to chew on it, too. Edmund took them both outside and I went upstairs to collect James's letters.

They were sitting in two piles outside James's door. One pile rubber-stamped YES and the other pile stamped NO.

I yelled, "Hi, James," and got back three raps that meant, "Hello, Annie." (Al-Willie's signal was two quick raps.)

"You want some food or anything?" I called and

got a note pushed under the door rubber-stamped NO.

"Okay!" I took the two piles of letters back down to Lola, who was sitting thoughtfully at the kitchen table.

"Thanks, Annie," he said. "Listen, you and the kids, you try the best you can to keep a low profile around town and at school, understand?"

"No . . ."

"It means you be kind of quiet, keep to yourself, mind your own business and be polite. Be nice to everyone. Tell the kids."

"Okay . . ."

"Because, Annie, we did leave St. Theresa's without discussing it with anyone and we don't want to call a lot of attention to ourselves. All we want is to be together and have a nice, peaceful time here. Right?"

"Right! Right, Lola. I promise, we'll be nice to everyone even if it kills us!"

Except there was nobody to be nice to, since no one talked to me. We timed our arrival at the bus stop in the mornings so that we got there just as the bus did and there was no chance for Molly to be mean to us or us to be mean back. Once Ben tried to reach for Orie's barrette as she was getting on the bus, but I saw it and grabbed for him in time.

At recess, Al-Willie and Edmund called for me and we went off by ourselves. Going home we made sure we were the last ones on the bus so we had to sit up front where no one else liked to sit and after a while I began to relax a little.

We settled down into a routine. After school we did whatever outside work there was to do, like raking leaves and starting a compost heap, or fixing a fence, or painting molding around the windows, stuff like that, to get it all done before the cold weather came. Then we'd help Lola with his work if he needed it before all of us would coopperate on getting supper. After supper was homework time. Not just school stuff, but stuff that Lola made us read. He was still dragging books home from the library for us and even Edmund had to read things, like *A Children's Cook Book,* with recipes a nine year old could understand and fix without the aid of a grownup. We never did buy a television set but we didn't miss it because we wouldn't have had time to watch it anyway.

We all had something to do and we all felt good. But it didn't last for very long because two things happened—one right after the other—and they were both bad.

8

The first bad thing was I got called down to the principal's office.

The whole way down there I kept thinking, what did Molly Stamwick say about me now? I didn't do anything except keep a low profile . . .

The Sweet River Elementary School wasn't very big, even though the kids who went to it weren't just from Sweet River, which had a population of about fourteen, I think. There were kids bussed over from Hattiesville, Raton, Altonburg and Toaz Hamlet. And still the fifth grade only had forty-three kids in it. So the principal could know all the kids personally if he wanted to, which I guess he didn't, since I'd never met him.

His office was on the first floor of the two-story building, and it was the only room in the school that had real wallpaper instead of yellow paint.

His name was Mr. Reedy and he was staring right at me as I walked in. He had both his elbows up on his desk and he was touching his fingertips together. He looked like he was praying. For sure, *I* was.

He said, "You must be Ann."

I said I was.

He said, wasn't Benjamin Beniker my brother.

I said he was.

Then he leaned way back in his seat till the back of his chair touched the wall but he still kept his fingertips together. I had enough time to realize, while he was leaning back, that it wasn't about me. Whatever it was, it was about Ben.

"What'd he eat?" I asked.

"I beg your pardon?" Mr. Reedy said, raising his eyebrows.

I said, "Nothing. Sir."

"Benjamin seems to have a problem adjusting to his new environment," Mr. Reedy said, and this time he didn't look at me but up at the ceiling.

"He seems to be adjusting fine," I said. "He likes our house a lot."

"Sometimes, Ann . . ." Mr. Reedy blinked his eyes very slowly and for a minute I thought he'd gone to sleep. ". . . when children are troubled, certain symptoms develop. They are only symptoms, though. The cause itself is deeply rooted in something else . . ."

I sighed. I wanted to say, "What'd he *eat?*" again, but I didn't.

". . . It seems that things have been disappearing in the kindergarten room. Only the *morning* kindergarten, you understand, and only things in the vicinity of where Benjamin happens to be . . ."

He went on to explain exactly how he and the teacher had narrowed it down to Ben, which he didn't have to do for me, since I knew right away it was Ben. What I didn't get for a few minutes was that Mr. Reedy and the teacher thought that Ben was a *thief*, that he was *stealing* things from other people, which Ben would never ever do! They didn't know he was just *eating* the stuff.

". . . I called you down, Ann, because I wanted to talk to Benjamin's sibling before I called in the parent. Sometimes a sibling can be helpful in dealing with certain kinds of problems, where a parent might be emotionally involved . . ."

I tuned out. I didn't know what a "sibling" was and I didn't care. What I needed to know was which would be better: to let Mr. Reedy think that Ben was a thief or an eater?

". . . a small money clip belonging to the teacher, a thimble, all of the beads for an art project . . ."

He was talking about all the things that were missing. I tuned out again.

I couldn't figure what to do. We all forgot that no one would be around to stop Ben from eating things while he was in school. At home we watched him pretty carefully without even thinking about it. Like, Ben's hand would reach up and one of us would shove a carrot into it. Or push it away. Or something. But in school . . . Oh, boy.

". . . coat buttons, erasers, the tail from a toy rabbit . . ."

Toy rabbit? Naw, that wouldn't be Ben, I thought, he's into hard stuff.

"Ben's not a thief, Mr. Reedy," I said finally.

"Now, Ann . . ." he said. He sounded as if he was talking to a two-year-old kid. "I've explained how we discovered that it was Benjamin who's been taking these things . . . Now I understand that there is an underlying cause, which has nothing to do with the actual stealing—"

I shook my head. "Excuse me, sir, but Ben's not stealing those things. He's eating them."

"He's what?"

"He eats little things."

Mr. Reedy put his hands down on the desk and I could see that his fingertips hadn't been glued together after all.

"We can watch him at home," I explained. "But we, uh, forgot to tell the school to watch him. He likes to put little things in his mouth. By the way, he didn't take the rabbit tail."

"I guess I'd better talk to your parents after all," Mr. Reedy said, standing up.

"I don't have any, but it isn't necessary, honest, Mr. Reedy," I said. "Just tell the teacher not to leave little things around where Ben can get them and have all the kids get their coat buttons sewed on real tight."

But he wasn't listening to me. He was mushing around in his files. He finally pulled one out. "No parents . . ." he mumbled. "You live with . . . your grandfather?"

Oh, boy, I said to myself. Out loud I said, "Yes, sir."

"And he's infirm?"

"No, sir, he's retired," I said.

"I mean, your grandfather is an invalid. There's a note to that effect clipped to Benjamin's file."

"An invalid. Yes, sir. My brother handles everything for him. And us."

"What is your brother's name, Ann?"

" Lo—Arthur."

"Pardon?"

"Arthur."

"You may go back to your class now, Ann."

"Yes, sir," I said, and began to wish that it had been something Molly Stamwick had said about me after all.

9

The second bad thing that happened was the cats' birthday party.

We didn't think anything of it when Edmund stopped coming with Al-Willie to get me at recess. He said he wanted to stay with some kid in his class and that was okay with us, except the kid he wanted to stay with was Aurora Stamwick, which we didn't know at the time.

Orie Stamwick liked Edmund right from the time they laughed over Molly and Ben and the housekey, but she told Edmund that they had to be "secret friends" because if her sister Molly found out she was hanging around with one of the "weirdos" she'd get killed for sure. So nobody knew that Edmund and Orie were meeting every day at recess. And when Orie found out about Edmund's cat, Saint Theresa, well, she fell more in love with him than ever.

It seems Orie had a cat of her own named Fuzzy whom she loved more than anything except maybe Edmund, so when Edmund told her about his cat, she made up her mind that the four of them ought to get together.

She showed up one afternoon at our back door and she was carrying Fuzzy, a black cat with one white paw and some white on the tip of her tail. When she brought Fuzzy into the kitchen, Saint Theresa stood up, arched his back and hissed loudly. Fuzzy hissed back and dug her claws into Orie's sweater.

"Look, they love each other," Orie squealed.

"Doesn't look like love to me," Al-Willie grunted.

"What would you know about love?" Orie said lightly. "Come on, Edmund, let's all go outside." They called Saint Theresa, who charged through the door like greased lightning. "See?" Orie smiled. "He wants to be with us. Let's go sit on the grass and watch them play, Edmund."

That's when they cooked up their little plan. A few minutes later, I watched Edmund head out for the shed in the back where he got the wheelbarrow and brought it around to the front of the house. Then I heard him come in through the front door, mess around in the hall closet, and leave again.

"What's he doing?" Al-Willie asked.

I shrugged.

That was the last we thought about it until about six o'clock, when Edmund came home carrying Saint Theresa. He had big scratches on his arms and face but he was smiling like crazy.

"Where were you?" Lola said, leaping from his chair. "What happened?"

Edmund continued to smile. Saint Theresa jumped out of his arms and marched over to the stove where he gave everyone his best sneer and lay down.

"Edmund, will you tell me what happened? Annie, go get a cloth and wet it with cold water. Al-Willie go get some Mercurochrome from the medicine cabinet. Now, Edmund, what *happened?*"

"We had the most fun!" he shrieked. Lola sighed. "See, Orie decided it was Fuzzy's birthday."

"She decided?"

"Yup. So we decided to have a big party for her."

"Oh, you did."

"Yup. So we got the wheelbarrow and the canvas sacks that we pick up your mail in?"

"My sacks?"

"Well, yeah, but we only borrowed them. I brought 'em back. And we went to find some other cats to invite to the party!"

"And the sacks were to—"

"—put the cats in. Right. Because they might jump out of the wheelbarrow."

"They must have loved being put in the sacks."

"No, they didn't like that at all, but we made up for it when we got to the school . . ."

"The *school?*"

"Yeah, we decided the kindergarten room would be the best place because it's all open and there are lots of toys . . ."

"Edmund, you brought cats into the kindergarten room—"

"Seven, including Fuzzy and Saint Theresa. Boy, did they have a good time!"

"I'll bet," Lola said, sitting back down.

I started to dab at Edmund's scratches with the wet cloth.

"We got in through a window," Edmund went on. "That's when we got the scratches, putting each cat in through the window. But boy, did they have fun!"

It sounded like it. They chased each other under and over tables. They pulled out all the yarn used for the sewing cardboards and dragged it all over the floor. They used the teacher's desk for a scratching post and knocked over a vase of flowers on top of it. They clawed the carpet and the kids' smocks. And they used the sandbox in the corner for a giant litter box. According to Edmund, to say they made a mess out of the kindergarten room is the Understatement that Ate Cleveland.

"Oh, Edmund," Lola said, dropping his head and letting it bang against the kitchen table.

"Wait till you hear what happened next," Edmund said gleefully.

"I can't," Lola moaned.

"What?"

"I can't wait."

"Well, we got caught. A fourth-grade teacher came back to school to pick up some test papers she forgot and she heard us. You should have seen her face when she opened the kindergarten door! One cat was hanging by his claws from the drapes and it nearly dropped on her head. Orie and I were laughing so hard she wet herself!"

"Well, Grandfather can't come to school," Lola said. "He's too sick. I'll have to go."

"What if they don't listen to you?" Edmund wailed. "What if they want only Grandfather?"

"We can't disturb the old man," Lola said calmly. "He's got a heart condition. This would kill him."

"Oh, that's good!" I cried, and then clapped a hand over my mouth. "I don't mean it's good that he's got a heart condition—"

"It's okay, Annie, I know what you mean. Now we've got two problems to handle. Ben's will be the hardest because he can't help his, but Edmund . . ."

"I'm really sorry, Lola," Edmund said. He stood

there with his head down and his hands behind his back. He looked so sad and awful, with his face and arms all scratched up. It looked a lot worse than it really was.

"Well, you should be. What an idea!"

"It seemed so good at the time," Edmund said softly. "And the cats had so much fun . . . Didn't you, Saint Theresa?"

Saint Theresa yawned, rolled over toward the stove and began to lick his paws.

"Betcha it was the best time he ever had."

Lola sighed. "Look," he said. "We have to find a way to fix this up with the school and everybody. Come on now, think. Because if we don't, we're going to be living with the town on our case, poking into everything we do and maybe everything we did before, too . . ."

"Come on, Edmund," I wailed. "Molly Stamwick's already spreading it around that we're crazy . . ."

"*Orie* doesn't think we're crazy," Edmund said, frowning.

"That's because Orie's crazy, too," Al-Willie said and Edmund stomped on his foot.

"Ow!" Al-Willie said, hopping up and down.

"Hey, that won't get us anywhere!" Lola cried. "Come on, now. Think of something!"

"I'll say I'm sorry, I'll say I'm *real* sorry," Edmund cried.

"That'll help. And we'll pay for the damages. But Ben"—Lola picked him up in his arms—"you have to try not to take things that don't belong to you and put them in your mouth."

Ben looked at him with big eyes.

"Do you think if we gave you a lollipop or something that that would help?"

Ben smiled.

"See, Ben, people get upset when you take their things."

Ben smiled again and Lola put him down.

"I'll go outside and play, Lola," Ben said.

Lola sighed. "Okay, Ben."

"And I won't eat any pebbles or anything."

"Good . . ."

"So gimme a lollipop."

I gave him one and he went out.

"Does anyone know about James?" Lola asked suddenly.

"Not from me," I said.

"Me neither," from Al-Willie.

"I never talked about him," Edmund said.

"Well, don't. That could be the last straw," Lola said.

We weren't there when Lola went to school and talked to Mr. Reedy. Mr. and Mrs. Stamwick were there, though, and Lola said they put the whole blame on Edmund, when it was really Orie's idea to begin with. After all, it *was* Fuzzy's birthday and not Saint Theresa's.

The Stamwicks said that Orie had never done anything wrong until she and Molly met up with the Benikers, who have done nothing but cause one disaster after another since they moved to Sweet River. The cats were bad enough, they said, but now one of them turns out to be a *thief* . . .

Edmund was allowed in for a few minutes to make his apology and that helped, but Mr. Reedy really calmed down when Lola offered to pay for everything, in cash, including a new dress for Orie, since the cats had ripped up the one she was wearing and Mrs. Stamwick couldn't get the dried blood out of it.

The Stamwicks and Mr. Reedy decided that they'd be willing to forgive and forget if nothing else was done by "those children."

Lola said he clenched his fists against his sides and smiled and said everything would be just fine from then on.

11

Everything was okay for about a week.
Then we brought this notice home from school:

* SWEET RIVER ELEMENTARY SCHOOL *
announces
ITS SECOND ANNUAL
EAGERLY ANTICIPATED
FUN FOR THE W-H-O-L-E FAMILY
HALLOWEEN PARTY
Monday night, October 31, at 7:30 P.M.
IN THE GYM
PRIZES * PRIZES * PRIZES

"Can we go to the party?" Ben asked.
"You want to go, Ben?" I said, surprised. Ben

never asked about parties or anything that had to do with other kids besides us.

"I wanna be Captain Terrific," Ben said. "And wear a red cape."

Lola, sprawled out across the living room couch, smiled down at Ben, who was playing with little cars on the floor, pushing them back and forth along a blue stripe on the rug. "You *are* Captain Terrific already," Lola said.

"I know, but I want to dress like him," Ben said.

"You *know*, huh?" I said to Ben. "What makes you think you're so terrific?"

But Ben and Lola just smiled at each other.

"Ain't you afraid he'll eat one of those little cars?" Al-Willie wanted to know, and Lola said, "Knock it off, Al-Willie," and Al-Willie said, "Aren't you."

"No, I'm not afraid he'll eat one of those little cars. Should I be afraid you'll eat one of those little cars, Ben?"

Ben shook his head. "Nope," he said.

"See?" Lola said cheerfully. "I'm not afraid."

Edmund, who was supposed to be practicing sewing-stitches on an old rag, mumbled, "No fair having secrets."

"Aw, Edmund, we don't have any secrets," Lola said, sitting up. "We just didn't want to make any announcements until we were very sure. But Ben hasn't put anything in his mouth except food for two days. Right, Ben?"

Ben nodded happily.

I said, "How come?"

"I'm not sure," Lola answered. "But I'm not questioning it. Anyway, we're going to celebrate. Ben, if you want to go to the school's Halloween party you can go and be Captain Terrific. Hey, Edmund, you learn enough to help sew a cape yet?"

"I can do two different kinds of stitches," Edmund said, "but I keep sticking myself with the needle. Even the cat scratches didn't hurt as much as this . . ."

"Well, keep practicing," Lola told him. "Who else is going to the party?"

"Me," I said. "I want to go as a princess. I've never been a princess before."

"Do you have a dress, Annie?"

"Uh uh."

"Okay, we'll buy one and fix it up. You'll be just as pretty as Auntie Lola used to be when she was a slip of a girl!"

Al-Willie giggled. "Boy, wouldn't everybody be surprised if they found out you weren't really a woman, Lola?"

"Listen, Al-Willie, if anyone ever found that out, there goes my job and our means of support. So don't even kid about it, huh? It gives me the creeps. By the way, what're you going as?"

"Me? I'm not going . . ." Al-Willie picked up his school books and started to back away.

"Come on, Al-Willie, let's think of something really good for you to be," Lola said.

"Aw, no . . ."

"He could make something that lights up!" Edmund cried. "He can do stuff with electricity and make a costume that lights up! Wouldn't that be *excellent*?"

Al-Willie didn't say anything, but he stopped backing out of the room.

"Edmund, that's a good idea," Lola said, scratching his forehead. "Let's see, what could he be?"

"An octopus!" Ben yelled from the floor.

"Huh?"

"An octopus, dontcha know what that is?" Ben asked smugly. "It has eight legs and it's green and it lives in the ocean."

Al-Willie's eyes widened. "He-ey," he said. "How 'bout that! I could make each of its paws light up."

"Tentacles," I said.

"Legs," from Ben.

"Aw, how can you make eight legs light up anyway?" Edmund wanted to know.

"First you have to make eight tentacles," I said.

"We can do that!" Lola got up from the couch. "We can get foam rubber and wrap green cloth around it and sew it up, right, Edmund?"

"Awwwww . . ."

"And we'll make a big head out of papier-mâché. James can do it. Can you wire it, Al-Willie?"

"Sure!"

"Fantastic. How about you, Edmund? What do you want to be?"

"A watermelon," Edmund said.

Well, we did it. I had a long blue dress that felt just like satin. Ben had red tights and a red cape that came down to the floor and he just loved it. Edmund didn't go as a watermelon. He went as an ice-cream cone. Lola made a huge cardboard cone and I painted it brown. It started at Edmund's waist and went down to his ankles, so even with slits in it he had to walk in tiny little steps. James made him a strawberry ice-cream top out of papier-mâché that just fit over his head and touched the top of the cone and he looked great. But Al-Willie was the best of all in his octopus suit. We attached the eight tentacles to a green suit-kind-of-thing made from a sheet and Al-Willie wired it so that when he pressed a little button under the suit, the ends of all eight tentacles lit up green from Christmas tree bulbs we bought. And James made him the most wonderful octopus head with great big cartoon eyes.

Lola drove us all over to the gym in the van. But when Ben saw that Lola was just going to drop us there and go home, he cried, so Lola said he'd come in for a while.

The gym was decorated the way you'd figure, with orange and black streamers and pictures of witches and black cats. There was a big pot in the corner where you could bob for apples, and on the other side of the gym there was a haunted house. The place was noisy and crowded with kids and parents and teachers. Ben put his thumb in his mouth but Lola took his hand and held it.

A girl in a Wonder Woman costume came up and touched my satin gown.

"You look pretty, Annie," she said.

"Thanks. *Orie?*"

"Uh huh. Didn't recognize me in the black wig, huh?"

"No," I said, but now I could see it was Orie. Her face was still scratched up under her rouge.

"Where's Edmund?" she whispered.

"He's the strawberry ice-cream cone," I told her. "But you better watch it if Molly finds out who's under the sprinkles."

"She won't," Orie said and pulled Edmund over to the table where they were serving refreshments: chocolate cupcakes with orange icing and guess what kind of juice with it.

"What are the prizes?" Al-Willie asked, nudging me. "Do you know?"

"No. Go ask one of the teachers . . ."

"What a marvelous costume!" a voice boomed at us. Al-Willie had just lit up and he'd pulled on a lever that made all eight tentacles stick straight out.

We looked up. It was Mr. Reedy. He had on a weird-looking putty nose but we'd have known him anywhere.

"Who're you supposed to be, Mr. Reedy?" I asked.

He looked insulted. "Why, I'm Ichabod Crane, Ann," he said. "I can see you haven't been paying much attention to your English assignments . . ." He waggled a finger at me and smiled to show he was kidding, which I was sure he wasn't.

"Sure, I have," I said. "Ichabod Crane from the Headless Horseman story, *The Legend of Sleepy Hollow.* We read that in the Valley Falls library, wasn't it?" I said to Al-Willie.

"No . . . Huntington, I think," Al-Willie muttered.

"Oh, yeah!"

Mr. Reedy snorted at me and Lola put his hand over his mouth and turned away.

"What're the prizes, Mr. Reedy?" Al-Willie asked.

Mr. Reedy twisted the putty nose and pushed it up between his eyebrows. "Well, there are a lot of different prizes. There's one for the prettiest costume, the funniest, the most original . . . One each, for a boy and a girl. And then, we have a big surprise."

"What's the surprise?" Ben asked.

"If I tell you, then it won't be a surprise, will it, Benjamin?" Mr. Reedy gushed.

"I'm Captain Terrific," Ben corrected and stuck his thumb back in his mouth.

Mr. Reedy patted Ben on the head and took off.

"Look, Lola," I said, leaning toward him. "That's Molly Stamwick over there by the refreshments."

Molly had on a long white dress with sparkles on it. Her hair was all in long curls and she wore a little crown on her head that looked like it had diamonds in it. She was holding a wand with a star on the end of it.

"I guess she's supposed to be the Good Fairy or something," I said.

"Some 'good fairy,'" Al-Willie snorted.

Lola said, "Mmmm."

Molly was with some of the other girls in my class but I didn't go over to them. I stayed next to the wall with Ben and Al-Willie and Edmund.

"Hey, Ben!" A boy dressed like a bum knelt down next to Ben and touched his cape. "That's a terrific costume, kid!" he said. I didn't know him, but Al-Willie did.

"Hey, Joe," Al-Willie said.

"Hey, Al-Willie."

"Joe helps out in my class," Ben explained. "He's in sixth grade."

Lola said, "Hi, Joe, I'm Ben's brother Arthur," and stuck out his band.

"Hi," Joe said. "Hey, listen, Ben, how'd you like to go into the haunted house with me, huh?"

Ben jumped up grinning and took Joe's hand.

Lola pushed himself away from the wall. "Ben, I'm going to go home for a little while as long as you're okay. All the kids are here, and your friend Joe, and I'll be back to pick you up later. All right?"

Ben nodded happily and went off with Joe.

"I get nervous about slips, Annie," Lola whispered to me. "If one of you calls me 'Lola' by mistake or anything like that—I just think it's better if I . . ."

". . . keep a low profile," I finished for him.

"Yes. Exactly. Besides, I don't want to leave James too long."

"James is thirteen years old. Besides, he won't even know if you're there."

"He'll know, Annie. You'll be all right, won't you?"

I wasn't so sure, but I said, "Yeah . . ."

"I'll be back in, what, an hour? Two hours?"

"Make it an hour and a half," I said. The kids seemed to be having a good time. Edmund and Orie were bobbing for apples, Ben was with his friend Joe, and Al-Willie was wandering through the crowd lighting up and poking kids with his tentacles.

"Okay, nine-thirty, then," Lola said and left.

As soon as he was gone, Molly sneaked up next to me with her friend Sue-Ellen Huffmier. I should have seen her coming with all those sparkles.

"Hello, Annie," she said, wrinkling her nose.

81

"What's that your dress is made out of, sleaze-cloth?"

"Keep your hands off it, Molly, or you'll be wearing it with me!" I warned.

"Come on, Sue-Ellen, we have better people to talk to," Molly sniffed, and they walked away.

I was bored but I wanted to wait until they gave out the prizes because I was sure that Al-Willie would win one, and probably Edmund, too. So I helped out by changing the records on the record player and pouring the orange juice for the little kids.

And finally, it was time for the prizes. The gym got really quiet and they turned out all the lights except one spotlight and that was focused on good ol' Mr. Reedy who was going to make the announcements about who won.

Sure enough, Edmund won Boys' Funniest and Al-Willie won Most Original, and even though Mr. Reedy didn't seem too happy about it, he announced their names, and Ben and I cheered loudest of anyone. The prizes they won were a soccer ball from Whipley's Sports, downtown, and a walkie-talkie set from Radio Shack. The boys were real happy right up until Mr. Reedy's "surprise."

". . . . And here's the special surprise I've promised you all—" Mr. Reedy called out, waving his arms wildly, just like Al-Willie's tentacles. "We weren't able to do it last year, since we were just starting out. But since last year's party was such a

success, and this year's an *even bigger success
. . ."* (cheers from the kids) ". . . we're going to
have the prize-winners' pictures taken, with and
without their masks, by none other than the Post-
Gazette. *and* the Associated Press!" (wilder
cheers) "Which means that all of you will be able
to have your pictures, not just in your own home-
town paper, but in papers all over the country!"

"What's the Associated Press?" Al-Willie asked.
He was standing right next to the microphone and
everybody heard him and laughed.

"It's a wire service. They send photographers all
over the world and they take pictures for newspapers and magazines," Mr. Reedy explained.

"All over the world?" Al-Willie said. "What are
they doing in Sweet River?"

Everybody laughed again and Mr. Reedy
grunted. "Well, my boy, we're a real all-American
small town, celebrating a real all-American holi-
day. That's pretty important. *Right?"* he yelled at
the crowd. The microphone shrieked when he
yelled and I clamped my hands over my ears.

"So let's turn on the lights and have the prize
winners get up there on the stage!"

"Hey, Annie!" Edmund called to me. "My picture's going to be in the newspaper!"

I smiled and nodded at him and then it hit me. I
gasped so loud I could feel it clear down to my
stomach and at the same time I leaped to my feet
and went charging toward the stage. I nearly

knocked over a woman who was setting up a camera but I grabbed Al-Willie by a tentacle and Edmund by his wrist.

"Quit it, Annie, you pulled out one of my bulbs!" Al-Willie whined.

"Come on. Let's get out of here," I said, heading for the back of the stage.

"Wh—why?"

"Because you can't have your picture taken, that's why," I growled at him. "What if somebody recognizes us? From St. Theresa's or one of the places we stopped at on the way here? After all, they'll put your name in the paper, too . . ."

"Oh, my gosh," Al-Willie said. His tentacles were all blinking. "Come on, Edmund! Annie, you go find Ben. Edmund and I'll go out the back way!"

I dashed off the stage, spotting Ben with his red cape easily in the crowd. I grabbed him and made for the front door of the gym, which was closest to me, but it's a good thing I turned back because I saw Edmund and Al-Willie being held on the stage by Mr. Reedy and Mr. Hawkins, the gym teacher. The slits for his feet couldn't help Edmund with running, but he was kicking like crazy as Mr. Hawkins held fast to the top of his cone. Both boys were yelling, which made everybody quiet down to watch them, and when Al-Willie saw a camera being aimed right at him, he pushed as hard as he could, knocking Mr. Reedy into Mr.

Hawkins, who had to let Edmund go, and the two of them raced off the stage and out the back.

I got out with Ben, once I saw they'd made it, and when we didn't see Lola's van out front, we took off down the road for home. Edmund ripped off his cone so he could run, but he left the ice cream top on and even while I was running for my life I had to laugh at the picture we must have made. A crazy octopus with blinking tentacles, two legs and a body with an ice cream glop for a head, a princess in an almost-satin dress and a little kid in a flaring red cape who kept yelling "Alcazar! Alcazar!" with his thumb in his mouth as he ran.

When we were about two minutes down the road, Lola saw us from the van and screeched to a stop. As we closed the doors behind us, we could see out the front windows that a crowd had started to spill out of the gym and all of the people were looking at the van, shaking their fists and waving their arms.

12

"No, kids, you did the right thing. Except it's too bad you couldn't have just slipped away, without all that commotion," Lola said when we got home.

"We tried, but we couldn't. Mr. Reedy grabbed me and Mr. Hawkins grabbed Edmund," Al-Willie explained.

"I know. Sweet River's Moment in the Spotlight. He had to have it."

"Yeah, well, it would've been nice," Edmund grumbled.

"I know," Lola said.

"We better stay home from school tomorrow," I said hopefully.

"No, no, that's just what you *won't* do," Lola said. "You go to school like nothing happened."

"Well, what'll we tell Mr. Reedy and everybody

who wants to know why we cut out like that?" Al-Willie asked.

"Uh—tell them . . . Tell them you just realized what time it was and you had to get Ben home," Lola said.

I laughed. "Right, just like Cinderella. We had to be home or the van would turn into a pumpkin and I'd be back in rags and Edmund and Al-Willie would be mice!"

Lola said, "Let's just hope nobody comes around tomorrow with a glass slipper."

We all went to school.

Molly actually left me alone. She kept giving me strange looks and I decided she thought we really *were* crazy and best not to mess around with.

Mrs. Weycroft, my teacher, asked me why we ran off like we did and I played it real straight and said my grandfather would have a fit because Ben wasn't home by nine o'clock. She just shrugged at that because what else could she say? Mr. Reedy had all of us except Ben in his office and he was awful mad. You could see it, although he tried to hide it behind a kind of sickly smile, but we just told him the same story. Poor little Ben, I said. We finally found out that the root of Ben's problems was that he wasn't getting enough sleep, and since we started putting him to bed earlier and giving him afternoon naps, he only put his thumb and his meals in his mouth. So when we saw how late it was . . . etc., etc.

Mr. Reedy found it hard to argue with. Things *had* stopped disappearing in the kindergarten room. It had nothing to do with how much sleep Ben got, though. Well, at least we didn't think it did, but who knew? Mr. Reedy had to let us go, but he didn't like the whole thing a bit. Not a bit. Especially since the picture that got into the papers was of Al-Willie's back, and the caption read: Kids Run from School Party! And there was a silly little paragraph about how maybe the punch went sour or something. Mr. Reedy wasn't happy. Uh uh!

Aurora Stamwick was the one who tipped us off about the committee. Actually, it was Edmund she tipped off and he was so upset when he heard, he wanted to leave school right away and go home to tell Lola. But Al-Willie and I figured the last thing we'd better do was cut school in the middle of the day so we waited until after we got home.

Lola was in James's room giving him a geometry lesson. James didn't object to the invasion of privacy once a day because he did want to learn and because it was Lola. The rest of us never went in at all, of course, except Saint Theresa.

Al-Willie sighed. "Well, we'll just have to wait till he comes out, that's all," he said.

Edmund shook his head. "Nope. I think we

should knock on the door. I think we should tell him now. We don't have that much time."

"You know," I said, "I think Edmund's right. Besides, James is part of the family, too, and he should be in on it. I think he'd want to be. Don't you?"

"I dunno . . ." Al-Willie said. "I don't want to disturb James . . ."

"We'll try. Come on."

I was the one who knocked. Lola said, "What?" from behind the door.

"We want to come in. We have to talk to you. It's important. It's about us and James should be in on it, too. We won't stay long if James doesn't want us to." I said it like a speech and held my breath.

Nobody answered for a few minutes. I was about to knock again when the door opened a crack and Lola stuck his nose through. "James says you can come in. It's all right." He opened the door wider and stepped back. "Don't crowd now . . ."

I held Ben's hand and walked in first. Ben looked around in wide-eyed wonder. Al-Willie came next, looking down at the floor, and Edmund brought up the rear, shuffling his feet. Lola nodded toward the floor and we sat down in a row.

"Hi, James," I said softly. "You look good."

James, in his desk chair, looked down at us. "Boy," he said. "Ben got big."

* * *

Lola said, "Well? Is it good news or bad news? No. Forget it, I can tell by the looks on your faces."

"It's bad, all right," I said. "They're sending a committee from the town to come over and talk to Grandfather."

"*What?*"

"Orie told me this morning right after we got off the bus," Edmund said. "Her parents had this meeting last night at their house and all the town big shots were there, like Mr. Reedy and a couple of the teachers and the head of the school board . . . Even the postmaster."

Lola looked startled. "Why the postmaster?"

"Orie said because he says you get strange boxes delivered all the time. He thinks maybe there's bombs in 'em."

"I knew he didn't believe me," I wailed. "Bombs! Oh, boy . . ."

"Orie sneaked downstairs and listened in. They thought she was asleep."

"Okay, go on . . ." Lola said with his face in his hands.

"They want to talk to Grandfather and make sure he's well enough to deal with us. You know, a good enough guardian. Because they think he's probably senile or something and doesn't know what all us kids are doing, like corrupting all the other kids in the town and plotting to overthrow the government."

"Wonderful," Lola said.

"They want to know what you get in these boxes. That ol' postmaster shakes 'em but he can't tell."

"I knew he shook 'em on purpose," Al-Willie muttered.

"You shouldn't shake deadly gases," Lola said and James laughed.

"So anyway, they're sending over a committee to talk to Grandfather and if they don't like what he says they're going to talk about going to the Child Welfare Board," Edmund finished.

"Did Orie overhear when they were coming?"

"Yeah. Next Wednesday night. They're coming here first, then they're going over to the church for a meeting about food baskets for the needy on Thanksgiving."

"Oh, great. 'Get the Benikers and Feed the Poor,'" Lola intoned. "It's 'Needy-Night' in Sweet River."

Al-Willie said, "What'll we do?" but Lola didn't answer, just kept his head buried in his hands.

"Are they gonna send us back to St. Theresa's?" Ben asked, reaching for the Scotch tape on James's desk.

Lola slapped his fingers lightly. "No, Ben. *No*. Don't worry about that. Edmund, go get him a lollipop."

"*Well?*" Al-Willie repeated. "What are we going to do? Because I've got this feeling they're not going to like anything Grandfather has to say."

"But we don't *have* a grandfather," Ben wailed.

Suddenly, James sat straight up in his chair, his eyes wide and sharp-looking. He reached out, touched Lola's shoulder, leaned in and began to whisper to him. We watched Lola's eyes get wide, too.

Then Lola said, "Nah. It'd never work."

"What?" I asked. "*What?*"

Lola rubbed his lips together. "James says I should be Grandfather."

"Huh?"

"He says I could make up like an old man and play Grandfather and show them what a stable home I run for my grandchildren."

"Well, it's a stable, all right . . ." Al-Willie said, nodding.

"Not that kind of stable, Al-Willie. Do you think I could do it? They've seen enough of the real me to know what I look like. Do you think I could fool them?"

"I don't know, but it's the only chance we've got," I said. "Considering that we don't have any grandfather at all, you'd be the best we could get."

"Well . . . We've got five days. It's time enough to practice."

James coughed. "I can help," he said.

"How?" Lola asked.

93

"I know about makeup. I'll tell you what to buy." He said it real quiet.

Though we all wanted to know how James knew about makeup, none of us dared to ask him, so Lola just said, "Get pencil and paper first!" and James dictated a list.

"What's 'clown white'?" Ben asked. "Is there going to be a clown?"

"No, Ben, it's white makeup that comes in a tube," James explained. "You can use it on your brows and lashes. Clowns use it all over their faces, but actors use it to make up like old people."

Lola looked sharply at James, but James was busy cleaning his fingernails.

"What else?" Lola asked.

"Moist rouge," James said thoughtfully. "Number Three."

"Number *Three?*"

"Yeah. And a very, very pale pancake. I can't remember the name of the lightest, but whatever it is, get it. Don't get greasepaint, that'll be too obvious."

Lola smiled at James, shook his head, and went on writing. "Go on," he said.

"Brown eyebrow pencil, a tube of 'erase,' a pale lipstick, and white shoe polish."

"Shoe polish?" Al-Willie asked, grinning. "What's that for?"

"His hair," James said calmly. "To whiten his hair."

"It'll smell," I said.

"No, the smell goes away. Besides, they don't have to get that close to him. They better not or they'll be able to tell he's wearing makeup."

"Is that all?" Lola asked.

"I guess so," James said. "For now."

"Well, we'll never be able to get all this in the local drug store," Lola said.

"You wouldn't want to anyway," James told him. "It'd be all over town in a minute. You have to find a theatrical makeup store."

"All right," Lola said. "I'll take tomorrow and drive to the city. I'll find some of it at least."

"Well, if you don't," James said, "here are some things you can get in any drugstore that'll be good substitutes." He began to write.

Lola shook his head again. "You amaze me, James," he said. But James didn't say anything.

The next day was Saturday and Lola took off early in the van, taking Edmund and Ben with him. Al-Willie and I spent the day cleaning the house. James always cleaned his own room. All I had to do was hand the vacuum in to him and he put it outside his door when he was through.

We had done everything but wash the windows by the time Lola came home. Edmund had made a tuna casserole before he left so we just stuck that in the oven to heat up and started to play with the makeup.

"Get your hands out of that stuff," Lola warned us. "James is going to do it."

"Ooooh, can we watch?" Ben wanted to know, but Lola said that was up to James, and went upstairs to check.

James thought it over and decided we'd better watch so he'd have some objective opinions as to how it looked.

"*Yay!*" Ben screamed and we all ran upstairs.

James put the pancake on first. It made Lola's skin look powdery white and pale.

"He looks like he's dying," Al-Willie complained.

"Wait a minute, Al-Willie, I'm going to blend something else in here in a minute . . ." James drew a line with the eyebrow pencil down Lola's cheeks and then began to smear it with his fingers.

"What're you *doing?*" Al-Willie demanded.

"Darkening the skin around the nasolabial folds," James said calmly.

"The what?" from Lola.

"The nasolabial folds. Don't move or I'll mess it."

"James, you really amaze me," Lola said again and I agreed.

It took James almost an hour to make Lola up to look like somebody's grandfather. Probably it took him so long because we kept yelling at him: "No, James, his eyes look weird." "Look, now he has no mouth!" "Hey, James, he doesn't have to be a hundred and eight years old!"

When he was through, Lola pulled something out of his pocket. With a grin, he held it up.

"What's that, a gray caterpillar?" I asked, and Edmund laughed.

"No, Annie, it's a mustache!" He put it on.

We all screamed. "It's perfect, perfect! No one would know you now, Lola!"

Lola smiled. "You think?" he asked. He looked like a skinny old man. He really did. James had used the rouge to redden Lola's eyes around the edges and the clown white to make his eyelashes and eyebrows almost invisible. The pale lipstick nearly blotted out Lola's mouth, and with a little of the pancake makeup over it, his mouth actually seemed to sink into his face as if he didn't have any teeth to push it back. He had dark shadows, like bags, under his eyes and with the shoe polish in his hair and the mustache under his nose he looked like he might have really been his own grandfather.

"Wait there a minute," Lola said, leaping up, and when he came back in, he was wearing a white flannel nightgown, old leather slippers and a real nightcap!

We all loved it, but James, sitting at his desk, shook his head. "No good," he said. "You look like the Ghost of Christmas Past. Forget the cap and gown and get yourself a pair of gray pajamas and a striped robe."

"Hey, this nightgown and cap cost me twenty bucks!" Lola complained.

James said, "Sorry."

Lola grumbled but he did go out and buy some pajamas a size too large and a robe made out of some thin material.

We decided that the people should see Grandfather, not in his bed, but downstairs, with us, so he wouldn't look like he was confined and out of touch with his family.

Al-Willie worked on setting up the lighting around the chair he'd use so that it'd be just dark enough and no one would be able to even suspect that Grandfather was only eighteen years old and wearing a ton of makeup. We set up the chairs for the people, the committee, just close enough but not too close to Grandfather's chair.

"The stage is set," Lola said when we were through. "Let the play begin."

"It's still only Saturday," I said. "The play doesn't begin until Wednesday."

Lola groaned. "I'll never make it through, I'm a nervous wreck."

"It's stage fright," I said. "I had it once when I sang a hymn alone in church. I shook like a leaf."

"Good," Lola said. "If I shake, so much the better."

13

Our big advantage was that the committee didn't know we knew they were coming. They had planned to just "drop in on us" and surprise us, but thanks to Orie Stamwick, we were more than ready. On Wednesday we had supper at five o'clock and were all in our places by six, because we didn't know exactly what time they'd come. Orie had promised Edmund she'd call our house and ring once when her parents left but we still didn't know when that'd be, so we got ready real early.

I was supposed to be in the kitchen washing the supper dishes. But they were already washed, so I just rinsed the same two dishes over and over. Edmund and Ben were supposed to be playing quietly on the floor with some little toys, and we hoped the people would get the message that Ben was no longer eating them. Al-Willie was to be doing his homework at the desk in the living room. No one knew about James and as long as he kept quiet in his room, no one would. And Lola— or rather, our big brother Arthur—was to have taken the van and driven over to another town to trade some stamps for his extensive stamp collection. (We hid the van about a half-mile down the road.)

When the phone rang at quarter to seven, all of us jumped out of our skins. It rang once.

"They're on their way," Lola said. "Oh, Lord, if I sweat, the makeup'll run . . ."

Al-Willie leaped up with a big handkerchief and mopped Lola's face.

"Easy, Al-Willie, easy . . . Don't rub it off . . . Careful . . ."

"I didn't rub it off. You look good, Lola. Let's hear the voice you're going to use."

Lola croaked out a pretty good old-man's voice. And in the glow of the floor lamp Al-Willie had set up, you really couldn't tell he had on makeup at all. Lola looked like an elderly gentleman in pajamas and bathrobe, reading the newspaper.

Even in the kitchen I could hear all the footsteps on the front porch. It was so quiet in the living room—even Edmund and Ben didn't talk or laugh while they were playing. When the front doorbell sounded I could feel my heart slide into the sink with the dishwater.

"I'll get it!" I sang out as we had arranged. I had on an apron and, keeping my hands good and soapy, I ran to the door.

"Oh! Good evening," I recited. "I'm sorry—we weren't expecting company. I was just washing up our dinner dishes!"

"Ann," Mr. Reedy said, "we'd like to talk with your grandfather if we may."

I wondered what would happen if I just said, "You may not," but I didn't. I said, "Grandfather? Why, I guess it would be all right. He's just here in the living room reading his newspaper. Won't you come in?"

They did. Only Ben's teacher, Miss Hollingsworth, wiped her feet on the inside mat.

Lola looked up from his newspaper with a surprised expression. "Good evening," he said pleasantly.

I felt a sharp jab behind my left knee and looked down to see Edmund poking me with a toy car. He was moving his lips and I bent down to catch what he was trying to say.

"Tea," he whispered harshly. "You're supposed to offer them *tea*. Or coffee!"

"Oh!" I whispered back. "Right. Thanks." I straightened up, hoping no one had heard us. "Excuse me, but can I—*may* I—get anybody some coffee or tea?"

"No, thank you, Ann," Mr. Reedy said, answering for everybody.

"Won't you have a seat?" Lola-Grandfather asked politely, indicating with his arm the chairs that Al-Willie had set up to look like they were there all the time.

"Thank you, Mr.—uh, Mr.—"

"Beniker," Lola answered. "Like my grandchildren. We're all Benikers."

"Ah," Mr. Reedy said. He sat down and the others followed.

"Ah, Mr. Beniker," Mr. Ward began. The bomb-threatened postmaster.

"Just a minute, Wilmot," Mrs. Stamwick said, brushing the postmaster aside. "I don't know if Mr. Beniker's aware of some of the, uh, difficulties his grandchildren have caused in this town. Because if you aren't, Mr. Beniker, I'd—"

"I've heard about some of the doings," Lola began. He spoke slowly and his voice sounded very tight. "May I ask your name?"

"Edith Stamwick. I was here before, in the summer. I brought you a cake. To welcome you to the neighborhood. But that was before my Molly—"

"—gave my little Annie rather a rough time in school," Lola finished. "A cake's nice, Mrs. Stamwick, but the rumors your daughter spread were hardly the warmest of welcomes."

Mrs. Stamwick said, "Well!" and didn't seem to know what to say after that, but the other people did.

Miss Hollingsworth: "Yes, it's true the frequency has been cut down, but certainly small things are still disappearing in our morning kindergarten. Why, just the other day, it was Adrienne Mickeljohn's barrette . . ."

"Jeez, he just can't resist barrettes!" I whispered to Edmund.

Mr. Reedy: ". . . A perfect opportunity to put our little town on the map and they just turned it into a shambles! The Associated Press and everything . . ."

Mr. Stamwick: ". . . Poor Aurora, just covered with scratches. And the kindergarten room was a complete wreck, wasn't it, Miss Hollingsworth?"

Mr. Ward: "Your grandson! Strange packets and boxes! Regular as clockwork! Naturally makes a small-town post office think twice. Can't blame 'em, 'specially after that bomb in the mail back in '68. Sorry to be so blunt. Rather be wrong than sorry!"

"You could be both," Al-Willie muttered, but only I heard him.

The head of the school board was there, too. Up to then he hadn't said anything, but when I found out his name was Mackel-something, the same as Mrs. Stamwick's friend who never said anything either, then I almost started to laugh. I wondered, since neither of them ever talked, how they got together in the first place.

But then he talked. I sighed when I heard words like "thievery" and "disruptive" and "nonadjustment." Through it all, Mrs. Stamwick kept nodding her head slowly up and down and her husband kept his lips in a straight line and stared straight ahead. I wondered what kind of a teacher he really was and what was physics anyway?

Suddenly, I felt a sharp tug on my apron hem. I looked down at Edmund, whose face was papery white.

"Look at Lola, he's sweating!" he whispered. "His makeup's going to run . . ."

But before I could do anything, I saw Lola pull Al-Willie's handkerchief out of his robe pocket and put it up to his face. Then he made the most awful sounds. They sounded like sobs.

Lola shook his head as if he were too upset to say anything and just kind of blotted his head and face all over with the handkerchief. I had to smile. He was pretending to cry while he was mopping himself. Finally, he held up his hand.

"I'm sorry to break down in front of you nice folks," he said and Al-Willie dove into his math book. "I'm just so taken aback by what you think of my wonderful kids here. Why, do you know . . ." and he went on to tell them about how we fixed up the house all by oursleves, which was true, and how we got the meals outselves, which was true, and how we all took care of each other "since we lost our dear parents" which was *certainly* true.

Miss Hollingsworth looked at each of us kindly

while Lola was talking and I figured at least we got to *one* of them, because it was hard to tell about the others. Listening to Lola croaking all those nice things about us from his chair in the dim light, I really did believe for just a little while that I honestly had a kindly old grandfather.

"What about the boxes!" Mr. Ward demanded, when Lola was through talking. "The boxes!"

"Oh, yes," Lola said, nodding. "My boxes. The ones at the post office."

"Humph," Mr. Ward snorted. "Not *yours*. Your grandson's. The big one."

But Lola smiled and raised his palm at them. "No, no, they're mine, all right. Young Arthur just picks them up for me, because, as you can see, I'm—" He touched his legs and his chest to show how old and feeble he was. "That's just one of the many kind and thoughtful things my grandson Arthur does for me . . ." Al-Willie coughed into his math book. "You want to know what this poor old man receives in the mail, is that right, sir?"

I had to smile the way Lola was making Mr. Ward look like an old snoop. Which he was.

"Well, I—ah—"

"It's my research, sir," Lola said and my mouth dropped open. I hadn't heard this part before. "Yes, I'm doing a biography on Noah Webster."

"Who?" Mr. Stamwick said.

"Why, you remember Noah Webster," Lola said as if he were about to add, "doesn't everybody?"

105

"Noah Webster was the famed lexicographer, born in 1758. Right? Famous for the *American Spelling Book?* And his monumental *American Dictionary of the English Language?*"

Mr. Ward said, "Huh?"

"Of course! It contained seventy thousand words!"

"Sir, I—" Mr. Ward began, but Lola cut him off.

"Research, young man, research. For my biography of this facinating man."

"Research?" Mr. Ward looked a little weird.

Al-Willie had a coughing fit and had to leave the room.

"Certainly it's research," Lola said heartily. "How would you like to read what I've done so far? Annie, why don't you fetch my manuscript," Lola said, waving at me. But before I could even gasp or anything, Lola went on. "Yes, I've already completed one thousand, three hundred and forty-two pages and you can have a good read out of it—"

"Thank you anyway," Mr. Ward said, holding up his hand. "But I won't have time . . ."

"Ah, you don't know what you're missing," Lola said.

"I'm sure," Mr. Ward mumbled.

Then Mr. Reedy stood up. "I think I've heard enough," he said. "We have some important business to discuss at the church, so—" They all stood up. I think the whole house settled with all our sighs of relief.

Most of the little group were out the door when Ben said, "Uh, oh!" out loud and pointed right at Lola.

Mr. Ward and the Stamwicks turned back and there was Lola, once again quietly reading his newspaper, with his mustache—really looking like a gray caterpillar this time—slipping down his left cheek.

14

"They saw!"

"No, they didn't. No, they didn't . . ."

"Sure, they did, man . . ."

"Lola, they saw your mustache fall off!" Ben wailed louder than all of us mumbling together.

Lola's makeup suddenly looked pale green. I went over to him. "Lola? Hey, Lola . . ."

"I'm okay, Annie . . ."

"Did they see it?"

"They saw it."

"So they know, then. That you're not Grandfather."

"They know."

"Listen, Lola, what're they going to do?" Al-Willie asked, beginning to pace back and forth. "Can they do anything? What can they do?"

"I don't think they saw it," Edmund insisted.

"Listen, kids, just be quiet a minute and let me think," Lola said softly.

"You want to be alone, Lola?" I asked.

He nodded.

"We'll go upstairs," Al-Willie offered, but he didn't move.

"Yeah, we'll go up to our rooms," Edmund said and took Ben's hand. "Okay?"

Lola nodded.

"Well . . . We're going," I said.

Nod.

So we left because there wasn't anything else to do. I guess we wanted to stay there and hang around Lola because he was like the glue that was holding us together. And we were really scared. But we went upstairs and I wrote a letter to James, telling him what happened, and slipped it under his door.

That night I had a dream. I saw my house, our house—the real one, right here in Sweet River. I walked through the front door and right away I noticed something funny: the paint we just put on was peeling. Not just a little, but a lot, great big peels falling off the walls like when you take the skin off an orange. And then, as I walked from room to room, all the work we did was coming apart. The sinks started stuffing up, the lights began to go haywire, and even the furniture—right in front of my eyes a leg fell out from under the kitchen table and the whole thing collapsed. And the eeriest thing was nobody was around. Even

James. Well, it's hard to tell with James, but when I pounded on his door there were no answering knocks or anything. And I kept running around from room to room, just watching everything collapse. I couldn't even cry or scream or anything, I just watched . . .

I woke up shivering. I quick stood up on the bed and touched the walls. They were smooth, no peeling. I got up and felt my way down the hall toward Lola's room. Those walls were smooth, too, and in the moonlight everything looked okay.

I opened the door to Lola's room and knelt down next to his bed.

"Pssst! Lola!" I whispered. "Wake up. Come on . . ."

"Wha."

"It's me, Annie."

"Wha."

"I had this dream, Lola, it was really bad. The whole house was coming apart."

Lola sat up. "Hey, Annie, calm down. Come on, sit." He patted the edge of his bed and I sat down. "It's not coming apart, Annie," he said. "Don't worry."

"But Lola, something's wrong, something's going to go wrong, let's get out of here, okay?"

"What do you mean, out of the house?"

"Yeah, yeah, out of the house. Out of the town. Let's split, like we did before."

Lola shook his head. "It's not like before, Annie."

"*Why?*"

Lola sighed. "It's just not the same, Annie. They really couldn't have found us when we left St. Theresa's even if they had bloodhounds. For one thing, they couldn't be sure we all left together. For another, we covered our tracks pretty well and once we got out of the state it would've been just about impossible for them. Besides, if we *were* together, they knew me, they knew us and they knew we'd be okay. They had a hard time with us, don't forget . . ."

"Who could forget?"

"Right. But here . . . They don't really know us, but they'd sure know who to look out for. If we took off now they'd have all-points bulletins out—"

"Hey, what's going on?"

Lola and I looked up to see Al-Willie leaning against the door.

"Come on in, Al-Willie," Lola said. "We were just talking about . . . our situation. Annie was all set to take off tonight."

"Yeah!" Al-Willie cried.

"Shhh!" Lola put his fingers up to his mouth. "Don't wake the other kids and don't worry them. I've got a plan."

"What is it?" Al-Willie and I both asked. If Lola had a plan everything was going to be okay.

"Can't tell you yet, but I've got one. So I want you to go back to sleep and not worry."

"What about school tomorrow?"

"Annie, you go to school tomorrow."

"Awwwww . . ."

Al-Willie came back to my room with me and we stayed up a long time talking. We didn't know what kind of plan Lola had but we felt better that he had one.

"Did you see Lola's face with that fake mustache crawling down his cheek?" I asked Al-Willie and began to giggle.

"No, I was out of the room then. I missed it. Was it funny?" He started to laugh, too.

"Was it! It was like a caterpillar . . . No, it was like . . . a *weird beard!*"

"A weird beard, a weird beard," Al-Willie sang and we began to laugh. "We could make up a song! 'The whole town peered at the weird beard . . .'"

" 'They leered and peered at the weird beard . . .' "

" 'They leered and peered and *jeered* at the weird . . . beard!' " Al-Willie was choking with laughter and I threw my pillow at him. He caught it and threw it back at me and I fell down.

Thump. Against my wall.

Quickly Al-Willie clapped a hand over his mouth.

"Sorry, James!" I called. "We'll quit. We couldn't sleep is all . . ."

Rap. Rap. Rap-rap-rap. That meant okay or no sweat or see ya later. Any of those. Kind of like "shalom."

113

15

They were waiting when we got home from school. Standing on the porch. A woman and a man. As soon as I saw them I knew two things: One, Lola wasn't home or they wouldn't be standing there like that, waiting; and, two, they meant trouble.

"You must be Ann," the woman said as I walked up the steps with Al-Willie and Edmund behind me.

I said, "Yeah . . ."

"Where's Ben?" Al-Willie whispered at my elbow.

"Dunno, maybe Lola took him," I whispered back.

"Who're you?" Edmund demanded.

The woman smiled at Edmund. "And what's your name?" she asked.

"I asked you first," Edmund said warily.

The woman coughed. "Yes. You did. Well, I'm Miss Roache and this is Mr. Ulbrich. We're from the—"

"Social Service, yeah, we know," Al-Willie interrupted and I jabbed him. That was dumb, they might be selling vaccum cleaners for cryin' out loud, I thought. . . . But I knew they weren't.

"Were you expecting us?" Miss Roache asked.

I said, "No," Al-Willie said, "Yes," and Edmund said, "Maybe," all at the same time.

"No one seems to be home," Mr. Ulbrich said. "We've been ringing the bell and knocking for about ten minutes."

Al-Willie said, "Well, then, go away," and I jabbed him again.

"What is it you want?" I asked. I could have invited them in but I didn't. We all just stood there on the porch.

"Well, actually, Ann, we would like to talk to your brother if we may."

"You may if he were here but he's not so you mayn't. I mean, you can't."

"Ann," Mr. Ulbrich said, leaning down toward me, "we have here some papers and we're to take all you children to our children's shelter over in—"

That was all Edmund had to hear.

"*Yyyyaaaaaaaaaggggghhh!*" he screamed at the

top of his lungs and began to race around the house. By the time he reached the porch again, he had his shirt off. Second lap—his pants. Third lap—underwear. When he was down to his one sock, he just stayed there, in front of the house, making awful faces and screaming and jumping up and down.

Miss Roache said, "My goodness!"

"It's cold out here," I said to Al-Willie. "Should we get him in the house?"

"No. He doesn't feel it anyway. Leave him alone. Come here."

He pulled me down to the end of the porch. Miss Roache and Mr. Ulbrich were too busy looking at Edmund and each other to notice us.

"Edmund's doing great," he said excitedly. "Now let's us do something, too, and they won't know how to handle us. They'll have to go away. Regroup. Plan a new strategy."

"Okay," I said and shrugged. "What should we do?"

"What are some of the neat things we did before? In our foster homes? Think of our best ones."

"Well . . . once I made believe I thought I was a lion and did nothing but crawl and roar for two days. And I'd only eat meat out of a bowl on the floor. Drinking water was sure hard . . ."

Al-Willie wrinkled his nose. "That's not so bad . . ."

"It was, too. I bit the people."

"Oh! That's good, that's a good one. You do that. My best one was throwing food all over the room, but that's hard to do here on the porch, and besides, this time I'd have to clean it up . . ."

"*I* know! Hold your breath till you turn blue!"

"Naw, that hurts."

"How about going catatonic?"

"What's that?"

"You just stand there with your eyes bugging out and your hands out in front of you like you were sleepwalking, you know? And you don't move and you don't talk. No matter what they do."

Al-Willie smiled. "Okay. Now let's separate. I'll go around the back and sleepwalk up to the front and then I'll just stand there near that tree. You start crawling and roaring right now."

He disappeared over the railing and around the side of the house. I got down on all fours and began to crawl toward Miss Roache and Mr. Ulbrich, who had gone to Edmund and were trying to grab him.

"*Growr!*" I roared, waving claws at them and baring my teeth, but they didn't notice me. They were still busy with Edmund.

"Come on now, sonny, please . . ."

"Now . . . we're not going to hurt you. Really, we only want to help—*ouch!* Oh!"

"What is it, Rowena?"

"This child *bit* me!"

118

"*Growrr!*" I said and leaped at her. She jumped back.

"Hold her back, Roger, hold her back!" Miss Roache shrieked, but I kept leaping and growling even though I noticed Al-Willie striding toward us with his eyes all glassy and his arms stretched out in front of him.

He walked right in front of Edmund, who still hadn't stopped screaming and hopping around, and stood there, staring straight ahead. I crawled around in a circle, panting and snapping.

"Hold it, now, hold it right now!" Mr. Ulbrich said. "You children stop this. Stop it this instant!"

I bit him on the ankle. He howled and jumped back.

"I don't want to get tough here . . ." he said, and Edmund began to roll in the dirt.

"He's faking. I know this isn't real, young man," Miss Roache was saying as Al-Willie stared past her toward the road.

Suddenly I felt two arms around my waist. "Gotcha!" Mr. Ulbrich cried and I began to kick and cry and struggle, but it was no use. He had a pretty firm grip and held on to me hard. All I could do was cry. He was even able to grab Edmund with his other hand. "Throw your sweater over him, Rowena," he said and Miss Roache did, pinning Edmund's arms together with the sweater sleeves. Edmund wasn't screaming any more, he was crying. And so was I. Al-Willie was still star-

119

ing. He didn't even stop when the van pulled up and Lola and Ben got out.

"Edmund, what—" Lola began, sounding frightened. Then he sounded mad. "What's going on here?"

"Mr. Arthur Beniker?"

"Kids, go on in the house," Lola said.

"They're from the Child Welfare," I said.

"We're here for the children, Mr. Beniker. We have a court order and we're going to take them now," Miss Roache said. "We're really very sorry, but—"

"No," Lola said calmly.

"We have the court order," Mr. Ulbrich said. "I'm afraid there is no choice."

Lola reached inside his jacket pocket and brought out a paper. "This is a 'show cause' order," he said. "I went to get it this morning and it sure took a while. But it's an order to show cause why I can't keep the kids. We're going to have a hearing. In court. And until we have it, the kids stay here."

"*Yay!*" I screamed.

Miss Roache and Mr. Ulbrich nodded at each other.

"Yes," Mr. Ulbrich said, examining the paper again, "this does supersede our order . . ." He looked at Miss Roache, who smiled. They were probably both thrilled that they didn't have to deal with us any more.

120

"Well," Lola said, "I'd ask you in, but I've been away all day and . . ."

"It's all right," they both said at once, and turned toward their car.

We all stood there, watching them drive away. Ben had his thumb in his mouth.

"Whew," I sighed. "That was close, Lola."

"Yeah . . . Yeah." He was still staring at the disappearing car.

Edmund began to walk around the house, picking up his clothes.

"Hey, Lola?" I said.

"Mm?"

"Everything's okay now, right?"

"Right. Sure, Annie."

"That's all? It's all over? They won't come back any more?"

Lola scratched his ear. "Well. What happens now is we've got the hearing, like I said. It's Monday."

"*This* Monday?"

"Uh huh."

"You mean, tomorrow's Friday and then there's Saturday and Sunday and then Monday? *That* Monday?"

Lola laughed. "Good, Annie . . . And do you know the other days of the week, too?"

"It just seems so soon, that's all."

"Yeah."

"Well, what happens there? At the hearing?"

121

"Oh, we show that we're taking good care of ourselves and we don't need anybody else."

"Well, we can do that," I said, grinning at him. "That's easy."

"You bet."

"And afterward, maybe we can take in another little girl, huh, Lola?" I hadn't forgotten about that. It was my new dream, like the one I used to have about my house that came true. "Huh, Lola?" I repeated.

"Go on in the house, Annie. Check on Ben. Make sure Edmund's dressed, I don't want him catching cold."

"Okay, but—"

"*Now*, Annie."

"O-*kay*. Come on, Al-Willie!" I called. "Al-Willie, you can come *out* of it, now!"

He leaped into the air. "*Yippee!*" he shouted. "Ow! Boy, am I stiff!"

16

We went to school on Friday, all of us feeling better. On Saturday, Orie Stamwick sneaked over in the morning to say she found out that the judge who was going to hear our case was a man named Donald Pink and that he was real nice and everybody liked him. That was good news. Al-Willie wanted to know how Orie came by all the information she always had and Orie said she just wanted to be on top of everything so she could help us out.

When Orie and Edmund went out to play, Al-Willie and I went into the kitchen. Lola was sitting at the table with a bunch of his mail strewn around and also stacked up at his feet; but all he was doing was holding his head in his hands.

Without a word, Al-Willie and I did the breakfast dishes. When the last one was put away, we saw that Lola hadn't moved from his position. I sat down next to him at the table.

"Hey, Lola . . . What's wrong?"

"Nothing," he said through his hands. "Nothing."

"You got—a lot of work to do?" Al-Willie asked.

Lola took a deep breath. "Yup," he said.

"Well . . ." Al-Willie bent down to look at the letters. "James go through these yet? Did he stamp them for you?"

Without looking, Lola pushed some letters at Al-Willie. "Those two piles he went through. That stuff he didn't."

Al-Willie picked up the pile that James had rubber-stamped YES. "Come on, Lola . . ." he said. "Take a look at these . . ." He opened the first letter. "Wow!"

"What?" I asked.

"Listen to this: 'Dear Lola: My father beats me, my mother ran away with the milkman, my sister's a junkie, my brother's an alcoholic and I can't stop drinking strawberry milkshakes. I weigh three hundred pounds and I can't get out of bed. What should I do?' Signed, '*Hopeful.*'

"Boy!" Al-Willie finished.

"Gee, how are you going to answer that one, Lola?" I asked, frowning.

He still hadn't taken his head out of his hands. "That's a crank letter," he mumbled. "I don't answer those."

"B-But it's rubber-stamped YES," Al-Willie protested. "How do you know it's a crank?"

Lola took his hands away from his face. "Al-Willie, it's my job to know which ones are cranks and which ones are real problems. If that letter was rubber-stamped YES then James made a mistake and I'll have to talk to him about it. Now if the dishes are done, go out and find something to do and leave me alone."

I looked at Al-Willie. He shook his head and frowned. I crooked my finger at him and motioned him outside.

"What's wrong with him?" Al-Willie whispered outside the kitchen door.

"I'm not sure. But let's see if we can do something for *him* this time."

"Yeah? Like what?"

"Well, why don't we take some of those letters and see if we can answer them. Or sort them or something."

Al-Willie curled his lip. "Well . . . it's okay with me, except we don't know the first thing about it."

I nodded. "I know. But James does."

"So what?"

"So we'll do it with James."

"Ha ha, very funny. I don't even know if James is still alive up there, for cryin' out loud—"

"Shut up, Al-Willie, he is too alive and you shouldn't be making fun of James just because he's an anchorite."

"Just because he's a *what?*"

"An *anchorite*, don't you know what an anchorite is?"

Al-Willie started to laugh. "Yeah. It's what you drop off the side of a boat so it won't go noplace."

I put my hands on my hips and glared at him. "*Anyplace*," I told him, "not 'noplace.' Anyway, that shows you how much you know. 'Anchorite' means 'one who renounces the world to live in seclusion, usually for religious reasons.' So there. It was in one of Lola's books."

"Well . . . the first part is okay. I mean renouncing the world to live in seclusion, but James isn't doing it for *religious* reasons!"

"Oh, yeah? How do you know?"

He shrugged. "James isn't religious. *Is* he?"

"Well, I don't know that he *isn't*. Do you?"

"No, I guess not."

"Want to ask him?"

"We're not supposed to bother him, Annie . . ."

Suddenly from the kitchen we heard Lola yell. "Edmund! Where are you? Come get Ben out of here, he's starting in on my paper clips!"

I ran in. Ben had come into the kitchen from the outside door and was standing wide-eyed in the corner with his thumb in his mouth.

"I'll take care of him, Lola," I said, taking Ben's hand, the one with the wet thumb. "Edmund's still out. With Orie, I guess."

"They don't wanna play with me," Ben complained.

"Aw, Ben, sure they do . . ."

"No, they didn't want to play hide-and-seek, they didn't want to play on the swing, they didn't want to play king-of-the-mountain, they didn't want to play dodge ball . . ."

"What *did* they want to play, Ben?" I asked.

"They wanted to play sit-and-talk. That's no fun."

"Okay. You can help us, then," I told him. I went to the table and picked up a big pile of letters. Lola didn't even look up.

"Lola? I'm taking these. We're going to sort them again, okay? Maybe we can help you with them."

He nodded.

"Lola, are you okay?"

"Uh huh."

"You sure?"

"Yeah, Annie, yeah."

I handed the letters to Al-Willie and went up the stairs toward James's room. I knocked on the door and yelled, "Hello!"

I got back my three raps.

"Al-Willie's here, too, James. He says, 'Hello.'"

Al-Willie got two raps.

"Listen, James," I said, kind of softly, "we need more than 'hello' today."

There was a long silence. Al-Willie and I nervously shuffled our feet. I decided I'd count to twenty-five and if James didn't make any move by then, he wasn't going to and we should go away.

I got all the way to fifteen when the door clicked and opened.

"H'lo, Annie," James said. "Hi, Al-Willie. It's okay to come in." He stepped away from the door.

"Hi, James," I said shyly. "I think your voice changed."

He said, "Yeah, maybe. We got a problem? I read your letter."

Al-Willie put down Lola's stuff on James's bed. "Yeah," he said, "I think we got a problem."

"I didn't stamp this letter YES," James said, looking puzzled. "Look, it's stuffed into the wrong envelope. Yeah, you're right. Lola seems in a bad way."

"We thought so. That's why we figured we better see you."

James pushed a bunch of books aside and sat down on his bed. "I guess he's worried about the hearing on Monday."

"But why should he be worried?" Al-Willie said. "All we have to do is show we're all okay. And look at us, we're okay."

"Listen, Al-Willie, you ought to know that what we think is okay isn't always what somebody else thinks is okay."

Al-Willie threw up his hands. "Okay is okay," he said.

"Well, let's *show* we're okay," I said. "Let's do some of Lola's work to help him out."

"Hey! Where is everybody?" The yell came from the hall.

"Oh, boy, it's Ben!" I cried, jumping up.

"You better get him," James said. "It's all right."

"Al-Willie, go find Edmund. This is a family job," I said.

"Ben, get the eraser out of your mouth. Edmund, read the next one," James said. We were all sitting on the floor of his room.

"Okay. 'Dear Lola: I'm in love with a man in my office, but he's very shy and hardly looks at me. I know he really likes me. What should I do?' Signed, *Mary J.*'"

Edmund put down the letter and looked at us. We looked at each other.

"Well?" I said, looking at James.

"It's a real letter," James said.

"Of course it's a real letter!" Al-Willie cried.

"No, I mean, it's not a crank. It's real." He reached for his rubber stamp, bonked it on the stamp pad and stamped YES on the envelope.

"Well, we're not through yet," I said. "We have to answer it."

"We can't answer it," James said. "That's Lola's job. We don't know how to answer it . . ."

"Sure, we do," I said. "Let's try." I took Ben's hand away from James's dish of paper clips and pulled him down on my lap.

"Okay," Al-Willie said. "Mary J.'s problem is she likes this guy but he doesn't pay any attention to her, right?"

"Right."

"So she wants him to pay attention to her, right?"

"Right."

"I know how to get attention!" Edmund cried.

"No, Edmund, no," I said and started to laugh. "She can't take her clothes off in her office and start screaming."

Edmund shrugged. "I always get attention when I do it," he said.

"She could play tricks on him," Al-Willie suggested. "She could hide his work or something."

"That's no good, that'd just make him mad," I said.

"Well, why doesn't she just say, 'Hey, I like you, do you like me?' or something like that," Al-Willie said.

"You can't just *say* that," I said.

"Well, if you're so smart, then what should she do?" Edmund said.

I thought. "She could send him flowers," I said.

"You don't send a boy flowers," Al-Willie said, smirking at me. "Yuck! Flowers!"

"Well, why not? Don't you like flowers?"

"Sure, but—"

"She could put flowers on his desk. In a vase. That's a nice thing to do. You think so, James?"

"I don't know, Annie . . ."

"But how will he know they're from her?" Edmund asked. "You gonna tell her to write a card or something?"

"Uh . . ."

"I don't like that idea," Al-Willie said. "I think she should just say, 'Hey, wanna go out?' Like that."

James was shaking his head back and forth. "I don't think we can do this, guys. I think what we have to do is get Lola to do it. He needs to be cheered up. Hey! Look at Ben—"

Ben looked like a squirrel. His cheeks were all puffed up.

I reached around and opened his mouth. "Oh, blagh! Rubber bands! Jeez, Ben—" One by one I pulled them out. He had twelve of them in there.

"Well, what's going on?" he wailed when I took the last one out and wiped my fingers. "How come Lola's sleeping on the table? Why are we in James's room? What's going on, anyway?" A big tear dropped down his cheek.

"Aw, Ben, don't cry," I said at the same time Al-Willie came over with a Kleenex and started to wipe Ben's face.

"Don't cry, Ben, everything's okay," Edmund said, coming over, too.

We sat on the floor together and hugged Ben and each other.

Then James got off his bed and walked toward us. He stood there above me for a second and then reached down and gave my head a light pat.

"Go downstairs, kids. Lola needs you down there," he said.

We got up and left the room.

Lola was still sitting at the kitchen table but he was all slumped over and his head was resting on his arms. The stuff he was supposed to do was still on the floor at his feet.

"Lola?" Ben said almost in a whisper.

"Hey, Lola . . ." Edmund touched his shoulder.

Al-Willie and I pulled up chairs.

"Lola, come on, cheer up . . ." I began.

He didn't move. There was an awful silence.

Suddenly, Al-Willie scraped his chair along the floor and hollered. "DEAR KIDS: I'VE GOT A PROBLEM! I CAN'T PICK MY HEAD UP OFF MY ARMS! WHAT SHOULD I DO? SIGNED, LOLA!"

Lola sat up laughing and he kept on laughing. Then we were laughing, too. We laughed until we nearly choked, and when we were just winding down to snorts and wheezes, we looked up to see James in the kitchen doorway.

"James!" Lola said. "What's wrong!" He got up quickly and started toward James.

"Nothing," James said. "Just wanted to see if you were feeling better." He nodded once, smiled a little, and ducked out, back upstairs.

17

Sunday night, I heard a soft tapping on my door. I went to open it, but before I could, I heard a sound. The kind of sound when someone's trying to shove something under your door. Only nothing was coming through, just the sound.

I pulled open the door and there was James, bending over, creasing down a thick envelope.

"Oh, hi, Annie," he said, and stood up, holding the envelope.

"What're you doing?" I asked.

"I was trying to put this under your door only it wouldn't fit." He held it out to me. "See? I wrote right here. It's for the judge."

"What is it?"

"It's a letter, Annie. It's what I have to tell the

judge. It's all here. And I want you to give it to him."

I took the envelope. "It got mushed on the door."

"It's okay, he'll be able to read it."

"Does Lola know about it?"

"Yes. It's all right, Annie, believe me. It's what I have to tell the judge. You give it to him. Good night, Annie . . ."

" 'Night, James . . ."

"All rise! Court is in session. The Honorable Judge Donald Pink presiding!"

We stood up and watched a tall man with a bald head and a white mustache walk in from a side door. Al-Willie pulled Ben to his feet. I was twisting the hem of my dress, the one we ran out and bought just that morning for the occasion. Edmund was standing straight as a stick with his hands behind his back. Lola was watching the judge and he looked pretty calm, considering he threw up twice the night before. Lola, I mean, not the judge. I mean I don't know if the judge threw up or not.

James was home. Naturally.

" 'Morning, everybody, be seated," the judge said and we sat. Then he looked down at a man standing near his desk.

"Well," the judge said, "what's on the calendar?"

"We have a motion in the matter of Arthur Beniker versus the Social Services Department, Your Honor," the man replied.

"Are all parties present?"

Lola stood up. "Your Honor, the petitioner is ready," he said. Gosh, Lola's smart. He was right. Studying isn't for school. It's for us.

Another man on the other side of us stood up. "The respondent is ready," he said.

"Who's that?" I whispered to Lola.

"The town attorney. He represents the Social Services Department."

"How do you know?"

"I found out how it works, Annie. Now, shhh."

"Okay . . ."

The judge was turning over some papers on his desk. He looked down at us. "You may step up to the bench," he said.

Edmund whispered, "What bench?"

I said, "Shh."

Lola and the town attorney walked up to the judge and he said something to them. Then both of them talked, Lola and the town attorney. Then the judge talked to Lola and he talked back for a while. I heard Lola say, "I'd really prefer it this way, Your Honor," and the judge said, "All right, then, we go on the record."

A lady with frizzy hair sat down at a weird-looking machine and started to type on it.

"I have advised you," the judge said to Lola, "of

135

your right to an attorney and you have chosen to act as your own counsel. We may proceed. Swear in the petitioner."

Lola put his left hand on the Bible and raised his right. Somebody said, "Do you swear to tell the truth, the whole truth and nothing but the truth, so help you, God?" and Lola said, "I do" and the judge said "Be seated" and Lola sat.

The lady with the frizz said, "State your name, address and occupation."

Lola said, "Arthur Beniker. River Road."

There was a pause.

"Occupation?" the lady repeated.

I could see Lola take a deep breath.

"I'm . . . a newspaper columnist."

The judge said, "Beg pardon?"

"I'm a newspaper columnist," Lola repeated.

"By which newspaper are you employed?" the judge asked.

Lola inhaled again. "I'm . . . syndicated. My column runs in newspapers . . . nationally."

"Under your own byline, Mr. Beniker?"

"No sir."

"Under what byline, Mr. Beniker?"

"Ow!" It was me. I mean, I. Al-Willie pinched me. "Sorry," I said, and looked down at the floor.

"Mr. Beniker, I ask you again, under what by-line does your column appear?" the judge said.

" 'Dear Lola.' " He said it loud enough. He didn't whisper like I thought he would.

There was a silence in the courtroom for just a

second and then there was a lot of noise. I looked around and saw Mr. and Mrs. Stamwick, Mr. Ward, Mr. Mackel-something and Mr. Reedy. And a few others, like the man who runs the hardware store and one of the post office ladies. Why would all these people be here, I wondered. I wished they'd all leave us alone. "That mail!" I heard Mr. Ward yell. "All that mail!"

"Please repeat that, Mr. Beniker," the judge said after he banged his hammer on his desk.

" 'Dear Lola' is my column. I'm . . . 'Lola.' "

"Mr. Beniker, you're under oath," the judge said, frowning.

"Yes, sir, Your Honor. I know."

"*You?* You are 'Dear Lola'? *I* read 'Dear Lola'! I mean . . . my *wife* reads 'Dear Lola.' "

Lola nodded. "I know, Your Honor. Lots of people read 'Dear Lola.' That's why it's a very good job."

The judge laughed. Suddenly there was a commotion in the back. I turned around to see Mr. Reedy, or rather, Mr. Reedy's back. He was headed for the door, taking the biggest steps I ever saw. Mr. Ward was following him.

"Where are they going?" I asked Al-Willie.

"How'm I supposed to know?"

"Very well," the judge said, banging his hammer again. "Order, please. Now, Mr. Beniker, I have read your petition and I would like you to tell the court what it says in your own words."

Lola coughed. I think the frizzy lady wrote that

down. The place was so quiet you could hear Ben chewing on a button. In fact, I did, so I pulled it out from between his lips and handed him one of the lollipops I had brought for the occasion.

Lola gripped the arms of his chair and started talking.

"I'm here, Your Honor, and members of the—eh, right, no jury—I'm here to explain why the authorities have no cause to separate me and my—the children.

"My earliest memories are of living in a kind of bar-restaurant. Upstairs. And coming down during the day and playing in the bar."

"Objection!" from the town attorney. We glared at him. "I can't see that this is relevant—"

"I'd like to hear anything that Mr. Beniker feels is related to this situation. Overruled," the judge said and Al-Willie said "Yay!" and I punched him.

Lola went on.

"I don't remember calling anyone 'Mama' or 'Daddy'—I really don't remember calling anyone by name. I recall a birthday party—mine—and that I was five years old. It was at the bar . . . and it was night. Everyone in the place raised their glasses up to me—I can still picture that—and I do know the date because someone said I had the same birthday as the first president of the United States. That was lucky because that made an impression on me and I was able to know when I was born.

"Then the bar was closed for some reason. The day they were packing up all the stuff, a lady fetched me and took me away. She said she was my mother and even though I'd never seen her before, I believed her. I didn't know then what lying was. And maybe she was my mother, I couldn't tell you. I know this sounds sketchy, but I really never saw much of that lady once she took me away from the bar and the apartment upstairs.

"She'd go away for most of the day, night, too, and I was left pretty much on my own. I learned how to make my own meals, basic stuff, you know, and I learned how to read.

"I don't know how I learned to read, I don't remember that. But I do know I could do it because I started to spend almost all of my time in libraries. We lived in Brooklyn, New York, and there were a lot of libraries around if you were willing to walk and I was. I just began to read things. Anything. Fiction, biographies, history—didn't matter. The encyclopedias fascinated me. They were my first books. The pictures! That's what did it for me. Pictures of things I'd never seen before. Places and animals—there was a picture of the Grand Canyon I must have stared at for hours. Pictures . . . They came first. Then I learned about the words.

"I think what happened was, I just stopped going home. That is, back to the place where I was living with the lady who was never there.

First I stayed away overnight. Slept on a bed in a department store. No one saw me. After that I stayed out longer—and more often. Finally I left Brooklyn altogether. There were places and things I had to see and I wasn't going to see them by just hanging around in libraries and some crummy walkup where the highlight of the day was what kind of soup can I could open up.

"I knew about school but no one ever put me in one and I never enrolled myself. I was learning a lot, all on my own.

"I hung around the railroad yard with the hobos. One of them I got to love. I rode with him lots of places on the boxcars. He'd lost a leg in the Korean War but you'd sure never know it, the way he'd hop those trains on the run. He was married but his wife left him while he was in Korea and he just never felt like settling down again after that.

"His name was Cory. He showed me Atlanta, Philadelphia, Chicago. He always had a bad cough and one night he just died. Riding a box car out of Toledo with just me and another bum in the car. I was eleven at the time, and on my own again.

"I developed a kind of carefree routine. I'd spend most of my days either traveling or holed up in a library in some town. There were always churches or missions or other kinds of places to get your meals. Or I'd beg. Sometimes I stole. But from supermarkets. Not individuals. I guess it's not much justification but at least I never hurt anybody. Never.

"My friends were the people I met along the way who had no friends. Derelicts, you'd call them. Bag ladies. Some kids. They all had stories to tell and they liked me because nobody could listen better than I could. And I guess these people had run out of listeners a long time ago. The letters I get—for the column—they talk of a lot of misery, a lot of pain, but I tell you, I'd heard it all before and more. How I felt listening to those stories I can't explain, except to say nothing surprised me any more . . . and everything surprised me all the time. Tell me how I could have those two feelings at the same time and I'll give you a cigar."

Lola stopped talking for a second and rubbed his eyes with two fingers. I thought—he's crying—but he wasn't. I could see it when he looked over at me. I looked back at him and nodded.

"One summer I stayed for a while in an abandoned warehouse, where all the kids used to go to get away from whatever they were getting away from. The ones that came there most often were the unhappiest. They talked about family problems—problems I never had. Some of them said they envied me and wanted to travel with me, but none of them really did. When I said I was moving on, they said goodbye.

"It made me think. The kids I met would tell

141

me that I was the lucky one because I could do anything I pleased. I wasn't sure about that, because they had families—people they stayed with all the time, not just for a little while. And people who cared about what happened to them, which I didn't have. I decided that the best possible world would be one where you could have a kind of family and still feel free to be yourself, whatever that was. So I made up my mind to someday have that, except it happened sooner than I figured.

"What happened was, I got turned in. I don't know who did it, but someone came to the room-over-a-garage I was calling home and my wandering days were over. I was brought . . . to a place called St. Theresa's. I was thirteen years old and it was my first real home.

"I could have left. There were no guards, and no bars on the windows. But I stayed. Not only because it was kind of nice for a change to be in one place, but because of kids like Annie and Al-Willie and Ben and Edmund and . . . well, kids who never seemed to be allowed to be . . . what they were. Just what they were, not somebody's idea of what they were supposed to be."

I was crying all the time Lola was talking, but nobody paid any attention because everyone was listening to *him*. When he finished, there was dead silence in the room except for me sobbing like a one-year-old baby. But I couldn't stop and quit trying to.

"Is that all you want to say, Mr. Beniker? Is

there anything further you'd like to present to us?" the judge asked.

"Yes, sir. No sir. I guess I'm through . ."

The judge looked up at the town attorney. "Would you like to question the petitioner?" he asked.

"I most certainly would," he said, and I wanted to hit him. He stood up and walked toward Lola's chair.

"Mr. Beniker, what exactly is this place, this St. Theresa's?" he asked.

"St. Theresa's in an interim home for orphaned or foster children. All of us lived there at one time or another."

"You stated that living at St. Theresa's was a 'nice change' for you. Did you like it?"

"It was all right."

"It was a nice place?"

"Yes . . ."

"Then why did you all run away from there last April 11th?"

The next sound was our hearts falling. I started to cry again.

"I'll repeat my question, Mr. Beniker . . ."

"You don't have to repeat it, I heard you. I wasn't trying to hide anything. We did leave St. Theresa's. But we weren't running away. We were leaving to get, to be, to stay together. That was the point. The kids were always getting separated back there."

"Your Honor," the town attorney said, addressing the judge, "five youngsters and Mr. Beniker, here, who was of age, did, in fact, run away from this St. Theresa's Home and School together. Four of them, and Mr. Beniker, turned up in Sweet River. The fifth, a thirteen-year-old boy, has yet to be found. I, myself, discovered this easily by checking with the Missing Persons' Bureau. They passed themselves off in Sweet River as brothers and sister. They are *not* all brothers and sister."

"That depends on how you look at it," Lola said. He looked down at his crossed feet.

I took Al-Willie's hand and he didn't even mind. Edmund pulled Ben over and hugged him. I hoped Ben wasn't understanding any of this because he'd probably eat the judge's hammer if he did.

"Mr. Beniker, do the children go to school?" the town attorney asked. Dummy.

"Of course they do," Lola said. "They work hard. They study . . ."

"But they haven't done well in school, have they, Mr. Beniker?"

Al-Willie stood up with his fist clenched, but I pulled him down. Lola said how our work was good but we had a couple of go-rounds with some of the kids and all. He made it sound okay, which it really was.

"What sort of supervision do the children have?"

"Well, I'm home almost all the time because I can do my work there, you see. They're clean, well-fed . . . We all share the cooking, but Edmund does most of it—he likes to—" Lola smiled down at Edmund, who grinned back at him. "And our Annie fixes the plumbing and Al-Willie handles the electricity."

"The youngest child. He has a very peculiar problem, doesn't he?"

Lola said, "Well . . . we're working on that . . ."

"Explain please," the judge said, so of course the town attorney explained about Ben's eating habits, which I was sure went over just great with the judge. And then he talked about Edmund and his tantrums—another plus for us. But Al-Willie and I, who were keeping score on our fingers, figured we came out okay on the supervision part (Lola was home all the time) and the studies part (our grades were good) and the personal hygiene part (none of us had lice and the house was clean). Only somehow, the town attorney was making it all sound not okay.

"I have no more questions at this time, Your Honor," he said finally, and Lola got up and went back to his seat.

"I'd like to call Miss Rowena Roache," the town attorney said.

I took one look at Miss Roache in a stupid pink hat and white gloves and knew I had to get out of there.

"Goin' to the bathroom," I muttered and dove for the door in the back.

Out in the hall, I just leaned against the cool

white wall and closed my eyes. I don't know how long I stayed there, but after a while Al-Willie came out.

"Oh, here you are," he said. "We were getting worried."

"So was I, that's why I left," I said.

"Yeah. You should've heard that old Miss Roache. She said we were all crazy."

"She *did?*"

"She didn't say 'crazy,' but that's what it came out sounding like."

"Rats!"

"Well, come on, you have to come back now. The judge wants to see us."

I held my breath and followed Al-Willie back into the courtroom. But that's not where the judge wanted to see us. He wanted to talk to each of us in his own office. His chambers, he called it. And each of us had to go in alone. That's the way it's done for kids under twelve.

18

We went in according to age, the youngest to oldest. Al-Willie and I had a discussion about which one of us was older and I won. I told Al-Willie I was sure I was born twenty minutes before he was, only I wasn't really that sure. I just wanted to go last. Besides, James was really the oldest, and I had his letter to deliver, personally, to the judge.

So when Al-Willie came out of the room, the judge's assistant walked me in, last of all.

"Hi, Ann," the judge said, friendly-like.

"Hi, Judge," I said back.

"How do you feel about all this, Ann?"

"Rotten."

"Tell me why."

"I don't know why everybody's bothering us. First time any of us ever had a real home and now it seems like all everybody wants is to split us up. I don't understand it. We're doing so good."

"It's not a question of merely trying to split you all up, Ann. Your welfare is the court's business. We care enough about you to want to see you in the best possible home."

"Yeah," I said. "I know. I've heard that before. Everybody *else* decides what's the best possible home for you. *You* got nothing to say about it. I mean, *have* nothing to say . . ."

"Sometimes children haven't had enough experience to make that big a decision for themselves, Ann," the judge said.

"Yeah, well, all of us've been in more homes than anybody in the world, so who's got the experience I'd like to know . . ."

The judge cleared his throat. "Ann . . . sit down."

I sat in the enormous chair he pointed to. It bothered me that my feet didn't touch the floor.

"So," the judge said, leaning back in his own chair and touching the tips of his fingers together. It reminded me of Mr. Reedy and I got a little sick.

"So," I said back.

He smiled.

"You say that you've lived in a lot of homes, Ann . . ."

"That's right. But no place like this. This is what I wanted."

"Why?"

"Well, because I'm together with the people I want to be together with. And . . . it's not just that . . . It's more than that."

"Tell me."

"Well, we're all different. And so we each do things for each other that no one else does exactly. See, it's like the parts of a machine. You take the parts out of the machine and they're just parts. They just lie there, they don't work. They're just nothing all by themselves. But you put them together in the right places and look, see, you've got a working machine!"

He was just staring at me.

"See?" I said.

He nodded. Big deal.

"You and Al-Willie are twins, aren't you?"

"Yeah . . ."

"And you did live together until you were how old?"

"About four," I said. It was the truth. I hoped Al-Willie told it the same. "Up till then we lived with our aunt, at least she said she was our aunt. Well, maybe she wasn't, but we called her Aunt Jess."

"Was she nice to you?"

"I guess. I don't remember. She wasn't so nice later, she split us up."

"Did you live in a house?"

"Naw, it was an apartment. It was on one of the high floors because I can remember walking up and up to get there."

"And what happened when you were four?"

"Well, these two strange people came to the apartment one day. They put a snowsuit on me. It was white and had this fur all around the hood."

"Sounds pretty . . ."

"Yeah, but I didn't have much time to admire it because next thing they were dragging me down all those stairs. I yelled my head off! They didn't even let me say goodbye to Al-Willie!"

"Was this a couple, Ann?"

"A couple of what?"

"I mean, a married couple. A couple who came to adopt you."

"Oh! Naw, it wasn't like that. They were just the people who were supposed to bring me to St. Theresa's, that's all. And that's what they did. It was a couple of *guys*, that's what it was a couple of. Two guys. They gave me a doll. When they left me at St. Theresa's, I threw it at them."

"Do you know why you were taken away from Al-Willie and Aunt Jess?"

"No, nobody explained anything to me. They just took me and left me."

"That must have been awfully hard . . ."

I looked at him. He wasn't mean like the town attorney. Maybe he'd understand. Maybe.

"Al-Willie showed up there. That summer. See, what happened was, Aunt Jess had somebody that wanted to keep him, not me. Only when they took me away, Al-Willie fell down the apartment stairs running after me and broke his leg, so he had to go to the hospital and he carried on so much, he rebroke it . . . So the people didn't want him anymore . . ."

The judge smiled. "Yes, he told me. He seemed to get a kick out of the story."

Then I could smile. "Yeah, he used to love to tell how he made a wreck out of the emergency ward . . ."

"So then you *did* get together again. At St. Theresa's."

"Yeah, we sure did. We screamed when we saw each other. Boy, after that, I wouldn't let him out of my sight. We ate together, played together and slept together. Sometimes in the night I'd feel a sharp tug on my sleeve and it'd be Al-Willie grabbing onto my pajamas to make sure I wouldn't go away while he was sleeping."

"And what happened?"

I shrugged. "Nobody seemed to want twins. At least, five-year-old ones. We kept getting sent out. Separate, Separate-*ly.*" I grinned. "Boy, I did everything I could to get back to Al-Willie . . . Sometimes I *bit!*"

"So I've heard . . ."

"And I broke things. I broke so many things if I had to pay for them now I'd be working the rest of my life! All the people said I was 'accident prone' . . ."

"You made them think you broke things by accident?"

"Uh huh . . ."

He shook his head. He had kind of a half-smile on his face. "And you got sent back to St. Theresa's every time?"

"Longest I was away was about a month. The problem was, every time I got back, Al-Willie wasn't always there. It was the same for him, too. But we kept trying . . ."

"Yes. Al-Willie told me," the judge said.

"We wanted to be together," I said again. "And now it's just as important to be together with my other brothers, too."

"I do understand that the five of you are very close," the judge said.

"Uh . . . Six."

"Pardon?"

I got up off the chair. I had to have my feet on the ground for this one.

"There are six of us, Judge-Your-Honor. There's James."

"Wait a minute, is this the fifth youngster that the town attorney mentioned?"

"Yeah."

"Why isn't he here? Why hasn't anyone mentioned him? Where is he now?"

Oh, boy, I thought. "We all decided I should be the one to tell you about James. See . . . It's very important to James that he has a lot of privacy. I mean . . . a *lot* of privacy."

". . . Go on . . ."

I thought, is this ever going to come out right?

"See . . . James needs to be alone. By himself. But he doesn't just sit around. He studies all the time. He reads . . . almost as much as Lola, uh, Arthur. And he works . . . He does Lola's work, he helps him out, he stamps all the letters . . . What I mean is the people in the outside world, they don't understand what it's like when you need a lot of privacy. They make James come out of his room and be with people and stuff and he just doesn't want to. He's not ready to, see? But with us it's different. It's okay with us that he stays in his room. We don't mind. And he knows he's got us when he needs us and we know we've got him when we need *him*. See?"

"Well . . ."

"Look . . ." I reached down and pulled the letter James wrote to the judge out of my knee sock where I kept it. It was a little wrinkled but it was okay. "This is a letter. For you from James. I don't know what it says, he didn't tell any of us what it says. But anyway, here." I handed it over.

The judge took the letter out of the envelope. It was pages and pages long. I stood there with my hands behind my back while he read it. No way was I going back in that chair.

I thought of looking over his shoulder. Reading what James wrote. I could have. I wanted to. But this was James's time with the judge and it wasn't my place to butt in.

"James is an articulate young man," the judge said.

"We don't think there's anything wrong with that," I said.

"No, I mean he expresses himself very well. And up to now, no one knows he's been living there with you, is that right?"

"Well . . . no one had to."

"James needs to go to school, Ann . . ."

"He gets all his school. He knows more than a lot of people."

The judge sighed. "Ann," he said, "thank you for talking to me. I want you to believe that whatever I decide it will be in all of your best interests, I promise you that."

"Okay," I said. He walked me to the door.

"Send Mr. Beniker in, please," the judge said to his assistant, and Lola walked in and I walked out.

Back in the courtroom, we all held hands. All of us kept asking Lola what happens next and he kept nodding at us with his finger to his lips. It was very frustrating. Finally, the town attorney stood up.

"Your Honor," he began, "I hereby request that the five minor children be turned over forthwith to the Department of Social Services to be placed in foster homes pending the final decision of the court."

"*No!*" It was Al-Willie who yelled first, but I was close behind him.

Edmund yanked at my dress. "Are they going to take us away from each other, Annie, do we have to go to—"

"No, no, no!" I cried, and the judge banged his hammer over and over, yelling "Order! Order!" Lola grabbed us all and said, "Shh, shh . . ."

Then there was quiet for a long time. Finally the judge leaned forward on his desk and folded his hands.

"The children . . ." he looked down at us and smiled, "have been in Mr. Beniker's custody since last April. They are content, they are being formally instructed, they are neat and clean . . ." (I smoothed down my dress, spit on my hand and pushed down my cowlick.) ". . . and I see no reason why they should not remain in the custody of the petitioner, Mr. Beniker, until my ruling as to permanent guardianship."

"What does he mean, what does he mean?" Edmund kept asking, but we could tell by Lola's relaxed and smiling face that it was okay.

"It means we can stay together until he decides," Lola whispered to Edmund over the noise in the court. He looked up. "Thank you, Your Honor," he said, and the judge nodded at him.

"Decides *what?*" Edmund asked, but Lola had taken his hand and Ben's and was walking quickly toward the door.

19

When I saw the door that led outside I started to cry again. I couldn't help it. I was so happy that no one would bother us for a while and so tired from everything that happened, I just wanted to go home and lie down. I couldn't wait to see my room again. And of course, James would be waiting to hear . . .

Only the day wasn't over. The biggest surprise was yet to come and it was right there on the steps of the little courthouse.

"Kids! Hey, Lola! Over here! Smile!"

We stood there in the glare of flashing lights, almost thrown backward by all the shouting.

"Over here, little girl! Hey! Look here!"

Lola grabbed for us again. His mouth was open and his jaw was hanging down. I guess mine was, too. Cameras, people—men and women with pencils and pads—a television camera and a woman with a microphone—

"This is Roseanne Ramirez at the courthouse in Sweet River, where today the world learned that the syndicated columnist known all over the country as 'Dear Lola' is in reality an eighteen-year-old boy named Arthur Beniker—"

Lola put his hand to his head. "That's it," he said softly.

I looked at Rosanne Ramirez, who was jamming her microphone into the face of a beaming Mr. Reedy.

"That's where he went," I whispered to Al-Willie, who was looking all around him like we were suddenly on Mars.

"Who?"

"Mr. Reedy. Remember when he left in such a hurry? Well, guess where he was heading for?"

"Where?"

I nodded at the commotion, the bunch of reporters and photographers and townspeople pushing and shoving and staring at us. "The world," I said to Al-Willie. "That's where he was heading. For the world. He finally got 'his little town on the map.'"

Home. I was never so glad to see it. We had to make a stop on the way to buy a box of Cheerios to give Ben something to do and he ate the whole box by the time we got back.

Edmund made Hamburger Helper for us for dinner. He was glad to have something to do, too. None of us talked much at all until after we were through eating and then we all talked at once.

"I should have known they'd find out about St. Theresa's," Lola kept mumbling. "I should have known they'd find out about *me.*"

"If I have to go to a foster home I won't do it!" Edmund kept shouting.

"Me, neither," Al-Willie said. "Me-ee neither!"

"Lola, did we do the right thing about James?" I asked. "Maybe if we hadn't said anything, he could have gone right on living here with you if we got sent away."

"I'm not going *nowhere!*" Edmund yelled.

"Me *neither!*" from Al-Willie.

"No, we had to, Annie. There are all kinds of things that can happen now, depending on the judge. They can come and search the house. They can make us all go to psychiatrists. Stuff like that. I can't take a chance that they'd find James without our telling them. Find out we were hiding him. No good. James understands that."

"Do you know what James wrote to the judge in his letter?" I asked.

Lola shook his head. "I know it was a lot. Your knee sock looked like you were wearing hockey pads."

"Yeah, it was a lot, all right. Took the judge a long time to read it."

"Whatever it was, it was right," Lola said. "It

159

was the right thing to say. I just know that much.
How about it, you guys want to listen to us on the
news?"

He didn't sound too enthusiastic.

"No," I said firmly. "I'm going to bed. Come
on, Edmund. Come on, Ben."

"I'm staying," Al-Willie said. "I want to hear
it."

"Annie, on your way to your room, ask James if
he wants to hear."

I knocked on James's door and asked him. He
yelled back, "*No!*" instead of knocking. I knew he
must really be upset. Poor James.

We didn't go to school the next day. Reporters
were camping out on our lawn. Big news, big
hoax, 'Dear Lola' turns out to be a boy. Big deal.

All of us except James gave interviews. Lola
said he thought it would be helpful if we did. Let
the world see our side and all that. He even let the
camera people inside our house so they could see
all the work we did and everything and how nice
it looked.

Some of the reporters were nice, too.

"Public opinion is running two-to-one for you,
Lola," one of them said. "You got the country behind you!"

The TV news made it sound kind of like a big
joke: "The little girl does the plumbing, ha ha"
and "The Lone Ranger hides in his room"—stuff
like that. But worst of all, Lola was a joke and the

people who paid him thought so, too. He got a wire.

"What's it say, Lola?" I asked, but I didn't want to know when I saw his face.

"They're sorry. They have to let me go, drop the column."

"You're fired?"

"They said I did a good job, but I lost my credibility."

"What does *that* mean?"

"It means people don't want to take advice from an eighteen-year-old boy. It was okay when they thought I was a white-haired old lady but the same advice isn't good enough from a kid. They're sorry, they sympathize. I'm smart and I'm dependable and I'm a good writer and I'm fired."

"But they knew you were Arthur Beniker . . . The mail was *addressed* to—"

"They didn't know, really, Annie. I just told them to send everything to Mr. Arthur Beniker. Anyway, it doesn't matter. I'm still out of a job."

That got on the news, too.

20

"Pssssst. Annie. Wake up."

"No."

"Aw, come on, Annie, we're due in court in an hour."

"Don't want to go."

"Don't you want to find out what's going to happen?"

"Yes . . . No . . . Yes . . ."

Lola laughed. "Make up your mind!"

"I'm scared, Lola."

"Yeah. Me, too."

"The judge seemed nice . . ."

"He is nice."

"But they were nice at St. Theresa's, too. And it wasn't enough."

"I know."

"Are the other kids up?"

"Yeah. Edmund was sleeping with Saint Theresa the Cat. He wants to bring him to court for the decision."

"You better let him. It wouldn't be good if he had a tantrum this morning."

"I know. I told him he could."

"What about James?"

"James will stay here."

"All rise! Court is in session. The Honorable Judge Donald Pink presiding!"

There we were again. Lola, looking calm but biting his lip. Al-Willie, clutching the back part of the bench in front of him. Ben, with a lollipop in each hand. Edmund, holding Saint Theresa, who was really too big for him to hold properly. And me, in my same only dress, with no fingernails on my left hand and about to chew off the ones on my right. I left my coat on the seat next to me to save it. For James. In spirit.

"Mr. Beniker," the judge began, folding his hands on his desk, "I commend you and what you've done for these children." He went on to talk about how healthy we were and how happy we seemed and all that, but then it seemed like it was all over for the good stuff.

He said being in "the limelight" wasn't good for us. He said we had "special problems" that needed attention, more than Lola could provide at this stage in our lives.

He said he knew Lola was out of a job and now had no means to support us. He talked about individual needs and stable environments and a whole lot of other stuff, but what he was saying all the time was: ". . . and therefore I reluctantly must rule against the petitioner . . ."

In other words, no dice.

"We lost?" Edmund asked, clutching Saint Theresa. "Does that mean we lost? We can't stay together?"

I could see it coming but there wasn't anything any of us could do: Edmund started screaming. With a yowl that matched Edmund's, Saint Theresa leaped out of his arms, scratching anything and anyone in his way. The people in the courtroom didn't know which way to look, at us and at Edmund or at Saint Theresa, who had already tripped Mrs. Ward as he ran under her legs and knocked over the frizzy lady's little typewriter thing as he made an enormous leap for the judge's desk and missed.

"Let's go!" Lola yelled above the din and in two seconds we were out in the hall.

"Quick, the back! The reporters are in front!" Lola said as he ran and we followed.

We ran down a back street toward where we'd left the van.

"That's why you parked so far away from the courthouse!" Al-Willie said, panting and running. He was carrying Ben.

"I didn't know if we'd have to go in a hurry. Quick, hop in!"

"But Saint Theresa!" Edmund wailed. He'd only managed to get his shirt off before Lola had pulled him out of the courtroom. "Saint Theresa's in there!"

"I know, Edmund, I know it and I'm sorry. But you have to make a decision quickly. Do we go back there for Saint Theresa or do we get out of here together?" He already had the key in the ignition.

Edmund sniffled. "We get out of here together," he said, but the tears had begun to flow down his cheeks. "Only later we have to think of a way to get him back."

Lola was racing the car down the street toward home. "We'll try, Edmund. But I can't promise."

I put my arm around Edmund. "Saint Theresa was a hero, Edmund," I said. "If he didn't cause that commotion, we never would have been able to get out of there like we did. He's the sacrifice for our family. Just like a real saint."

"Yeah," Al-Willie said. "You should be proud of him."

Edmund smiled even though he was still crying. "Yeah," he said. "A real saint. I told you."

* * *

The van screeched as we pulled into the driveway. We had our instructions: Each rush in, grab one small bag, put our most important things in it, and get back out to the van.

Once inside the front door we got a big surprise. James was standing there.

"They've gotta be right behind us," Lola said, heading for the stairs. "Get your stuff *fast!*"

"No! Lola!" James cried. "It's all here . . ."

There were six little gym bags in the living room.

"I packed. For everybody."

We all climbed back into the van in what seemed like double time.

"Everything important is right here in this van," Lola said, starting it up again. We pulled out and headed away from town toward the highway.

"Siren!" Ben yelled. "Siren!"

"The lollipops are in the green bag!" James cried.

"Got it!" Edmund said. He unzipped it, got one out and handed it to Ben.

"It's all right," Lola said. "If it's going toward our house from town, we're going the other way."

"Didn't you say we couldn't do this, Lola? Before, when I wanted to go?" I asked.

"Yeah."

"Well, won't they catch us? Now they know who we are and everything?"

167

Lola rubbed his forehead and didn't answer.

"Lola, are you crying?" I asked, peering at him. He just kept driving.

"We had to try it the legal way, Annie," James said quietly. "If it could've worked out, it would've been better."

"Will they catch us?" I asked again.

"Well," James said, "I brought the makeup . . ."

Al-Willie laughed. "We'll all be disguised!"

"And I put two gallons of paint in the van last night," James said, sounding triumphant.

"Paint? What for?" Al-Willie asked.

"To paint the van, Al-Willie, what else?" Lola said. He was grinning. "When we find a good place to pull over for lunch, we'll paint the van. What should we paint on it?"

"Flowers!" I cried.

"Aw, *flowers!*" from Al-Willie.

When we were far enough out of town, we stopped at a roadside delicatessen and got sandwiches. But we didn't stay there. We drove on some more before we stopped. When we found some woods, we pulled the van off the road, ate the sandwiches and painted the van. Pale green. With one flower on the back.

"Doesn't look anything like it did before," I said.

"No, but we'll have to get rid of it after a while," Lola said. "Because of the license plate.

But it's a good van. We can maybe trade it with someone for an old truck or something."

Back in the van. James went into a little corner of his own near the rear door. Everyone else moved up a little to give him some space. Everyone except me.

"James?" I tried to whisper so no one else could hear.

"What?"

"Can I ask you something?"

"Yeah . . ." he frowned. "I don't know if I'll answer you, though . . ."

"Could you just tell me something, James? Could you just tell me if you told the judge your life story?"

James tilted his head. "Why do you want to know that?"

"Because there's something that's really been bothering me. Well, not exactly bothering me, but it's driving me nuts."

"What?"

"I always wanted to know how you knew so much about, you know, makeup. And stage things. I figured if you could tell that old stranger-judge your life story, then maybe you wouldn't mind so much telling me that one little thing."

James shifted his position. " 'That one little thing' *is* practically my life story, Annie . . ."

"I don't want to butt in, James, except . . . I mean . . . were you a *movie star* or something?"

169

James snorted. "Naw, Annie, nothing like that."

I had an idea. "Look. You know the stamps you used on Lola's mail? YES and NO?"

"Yeah . . ."

"Did you bring 'em?"

"Yeah . . ." He touched the green bag. "They're in here. Why?"

"Well, how about if I ask you Twenty Questions, and you can stamp the answers if you don't want to talk?"

James pushed the green bag aside and shook his head. "Look, Annie . . . I was born in a carnival. I didn't know my father, my mother did a trapeze thing. It was a traveling show . . ."

"Gosh!"

"It wasn't glamorous, it was a cheap carny and it was more cramped and crowded and smelly than you could ever believe."

"And that's where you learned about makeup and stuff?"

"Yeah. Clowns . . . my mother . . . everybody. Some of the carny kids liked it, but I never did."

"So you left."

"No. I *got* left. My mother married the owner of the carny. He gave her a solo spot in the show and they both gave *me* to St. Theresa's."

"Boy. So here you are, cramped and traveling again . . ." I waved my hand around the back of the van.

"No, Annie . . ." James smiled. "This is a lot different."

* * *

Before the sun went down, we had clocked three hundred miles. Not bad, considering the time it took to paint the van.

We were on an open two-lane highway with no other car on the road and we were just about to pull over to sleep. Edmund, Al-Willie, Ben and James were already asleep. I stayed up to keep Lola company while he drove.

Suddenly, my eyes opened wide.

"Stop, Lola! Stop the car!"

"Annie, what—"

"Whazzamatter?" Al-Willie asked sleepily.

"*Stop!*"

Lola stopped.

"See? See her?"

"Who!"

"That kid over there! Didn't you see her thumbing a ride?"

Lola squinted and stared at where I was pointing. "My gosh, Annie, she's lying down leaning against the fence. How could anybody have seen that?"

"I did," I said. "It's a little kid, all alone, thumbing a ride."

Lola and Al-Willie and I got out of the car and walked over to the kid. She was still leaning against the fence with her thumb out, grinning at us.

I said, "Hi!"

"Hya," she said back.

"Are you a runaway?"

"Yup. But not from any folks. From a school. For kids that nobody wants."

I looked at Lola who looked at Al-Willie who looked back at me. We all smiled.

"What's your name?" I asked.

"Yolanda," she said.

"Where you going, Yolanda?" Lola asked.

"Anywhere," she answered, still grinning.

"How old are you?" I asked.

"Almost eleven."

"Us, too," I said, pointing to Al-Willie and myself. "Listen, Yolanda . . . *we're* going . . . anywhere."

"Then we're going to the same place," she answered, getting up.

"Yolanda!" Al-Willie said to himself. "What an excellent name!"

"Hey, Annie!" Lola said with a big smile.

"What're *you* grinning at?" I said, beginning to smile myself.

"Congratulations—it's a girl!"

What Happened to Us

Sometimes I wish they could see us—Mr. and Mrs. Stamwick and Mr. Ward and Molly and especially Mr. Reedy. We're all a year older and we've grown a lot! Al-Willie is at least two inches taller than I am but I'm doing stretching exercises to catch up. It is a big joke, measuring us against the fruit trees every morning. We are all so tan, so much darker than we were even last summer in Sweet River, except for Yolanda, who was black to begin with.

After we found and adopted her, we kept on heading west until we got to the end of west—California. We traded the pale green van with the flower on the back for another one in Kansas and we traded that one for an old pickup truck with a

173

top on it in Utah, right at the border of Nevada. We stayed "under cover," Lola grew a beard, and we never had any trouble from anybody.

We still spent days in libraries, just like we used to, and Lola saw to it that we kept up with all our studies. He still does. He teaches us and the other traveling kids, too, if they want it. We've been moving around California for a few months now, picking fruit, living on farms, and moving on. And we all love it.

Lola fixed up an office in the back of the truck. It has a little table-desk kind of thing with a clunky typewriter on it. During the day, James uses it. He's studying and practicing to write an advice column of his own, only for kids, not for grownups. It'll be called "Dear James," of course, and pretty soon he'll be ready to send out samples along with a resume he made up. Lola's helping him and I know he'll be good at it.

Lola picks peaches and oranges and stuff with us during the day, and he uses the office at night, where he's writing his book that he calls his "memwahrs." He says it's about his life and his job being "Dear Lola" and about us as a family. Al-Willie says nobody'd believe it.

We had to get used to calling Lola "Art," since he's not really "Lola" any more and besides, the name "Lola" probably wouldn't sit too well with Jeanette Hostetler, who's his girlfriend. She's seventeen years old, and we work a lot of the same farms. When Lola's not writing his book, he goes out with Jeanette in her father's truck. Al-Willie likes her, but I think she giggles too much.

Edmund finally stopped talking about Saint Theresa when we got him a rabbit. He named it Aurora, after Orie Stamwick. Funny about Edmund. We met a lot of Mexican kids picking fruit, and Edmund right off started talking Spanish with them. Turned out Edmund is half-Puerto Rican. I said to him, "How come you never spoke Spanish to us?" and Edmund said back, "You wouldn't have understood me!" which was true, of course. Anyway, he said he'd forgotten a lot of it, but now it's come back and he's teaching us how to speak it, too. Some of the words he remembers, though, Lola says we can do without.

Ben is six years old and really terrific. He is on a complete fruit and vegetable diet and that's all he eats! Except for sometimes rice and potatoes. And he can read and write and play gin rummy.

Yolanda's a very nice sister to me. She never had any kind of family before, so ours is just as special to her as it is to us. Lola got her books on auto mechanics and if ever anything's wrong with the truck, Yolanda can usually fix it. She can also sew and knit and she's teaching me. I made a pair of purple socks for Al-Willie that he keeps his loose change in.

* * *

175

We don't think about getting caught any more. People don't pay much attention to us—we're just part of a group of folks all doing pretty much the same thing. But if we ever do get caught, what we'll do is go to court again. Every state is different and every judge is different and—well, we'll just try it again. Someday we'll be old enough so nobody'll bother us, and then—maybe, we'll make families of our own, where all the kids are wanted. My new dream is a family reunion at Christmas time, with all of us! We'd have to rent out a barn! Someday.

I wrote a letter to "Dear Lola." Not the column, just for Lola himself. I haven't given it to him yet, but when I do, maybe he'd want to put it in his book. It goes:

> *Dear Lola:*
> *You're the best Mom and Dad*
> *We could ever have had.*
>
> > *All my love,*
> > *Annie*